Beltaine Fire

Griffon sat with an elbow resting on his knee, propped against the lichen-covered stones of the Druid well. An early morning mist crept through the dense undergrowth bringing with it the pungent odors of the conifer forest. The morning chill still clung to the air. Weak streaks of a pale dawn tried, in vain, to penetrate the dense canopy of the forest. Heavy black clouds seemed to hang just out of reach of the towering treetops. It would rain soon. His gaze strayed, not for the first time, back to the woman. He had found her here in the early dawn hours, at the very spot of which Adolphus had spoken.

She lay upon a bed of moss at the foot of the Druid well. To find a woman alone in this wild, remote place, a place of secrets and rituals, should have seemed uncommon strange. But Griffon found it pleased him immensely. Though he could not say why he found it so. A small break in the clouds sent a shaft of brilliant sunlight down to play among the trees. Griffon watched small rainbows form in the mist rising from the forest floor. A sigh again brought his attention back to the woman. Sleep did not appear to comfort her because twice she had cried out softly, one small white hand raised vaguely to ward off some unseen blow.

What They Are Saying About
Beltaine Fire

"…Debut author, Katherine McGibbons has given us a gift with Beltaine Fire. Her heroine may have studied ancient Ireland in college, but she takes an actual ringside seat at Dun Tirlough in 678 AD. She meets the inhabitants personally and *you* get to come along.

Without revealing too much of the story, I simply want to encourage you to pick up Beltaine Fire and read it for yourself. Ms. McGibbons has a wonderfully descriptive writing style that lets you view the Irish countryside as though you were there on the very spot. I swear I could smell the wild flowers and feel the fresh air on my face. The story is exciting and draws you in from the beginning, and it only gets better with each page you turn. So treat yourself to a great fantasy read. When you finish, I'll bet you'll join me in looking for future releases by this great new author."

—Brett Scott
Crystal Review

Wings

Beltaine Fire

by

Kathrine McGibbons

A Wings ePress, Inc.

Fantasy Time-Travel Romance Novel

Wings ePress, Inc.

Edited by: Elizabeth Struble
Copy Edited by: Leslie Hodges
Senior Editor: Elizabeth Struble
Managing Editor: Leslie Hodges
Executive Editor: Lorraine Stephens
Cover Artist: Pam Ripling

Wings ePress Books
http://www.wings-press.com

Copyright © 2004 by Cathy J. Jurado
ISBN 1-59088-720-4

Published In the United States Of America

August 2004

Wings ePress Inc.
403 Wallace Court
Richmond, KY 40475

Dedication

Believing in yourself is not always an easy thing to do, and the journey through life is difficult enough without adding self-doubt into the mix. Having friends and family who believe in you makes the journey that much easier. This novel is dedicated to several people; my mother, Rosaline, and my step-father, Curtis, who never doubted that I would succeed.

To my friends; Ginger and Kay, who gave me as much encouragement as I needed to see this through, sometime giving me just that little extra push that was needed to continue on.

Finally, my husband, Jerry, who has been so supportive throughout all these years. He gave me everything I needed to make this novel come to fruition. Without his support and encouragement, I would never have made it to this point, and this novel would never have seen the light of day.

Prologue

Dun Tirlough, Eire in the year of our Lord, 678

Connault, Lord of Dun Tirlough, warlord to King Brennus, lay in the bed he shared with his Lady Wife, Boann, for the thirty years of their marriage. The chamber had been dimmed against the bright sunlight, which seeks to stream through the narrow openings that serve as windows in the thick stone walls. Rich, thick tapestries pulled tight across wooden frames are swung across the windows and would indeed have plunged the chamber into deepest darkness if not for the mellow flicker of light cast by the braziers standing in each corner. Lord Connault lay abed, though not quietly. Each of Connault's household had been called into his presence, given instruction or admonition, whichever the old lord had deemed needed and often emphasized by the pounding of the ale horn clutched in his meaty fist upon the low table to his left. The gray-green pallor of his skin belied the vigorous and virile good health that had been so recently his. Connault gathered his household to his bedchamber so they might witness his passing over to the otherworld, though he saw no reason to allow his passing to interfere with his rule over his clan.

Griffon, the youngest of Connault's sons, moved to his lord's side, his paternity evident only in his towering height and the broad, muscular set of his shoulders and arms. His dark coloring and gray eyes speak of his mother Boann's blood, as does his otherwise slender build. Griffon is a well-formed man of twenty and four years. He is much favored by the young women of the clan, but has a brooding look to his storm-gray eyes. This is not inappropriate while standing at the deathbed of his Lord and father, though it had been too often present since the death of his young wife three years earlier.

Also present at his father's side stands Bryon, Connault's eldest living son and heir to his place at the king's court. Connault's paternity is more evidently stamped upon this son, Bryon having the same fire-red hair as well as the blue eyes of his father, though he is clean-shaven in the Roman fashion, unlike his full-bearded father. Connault's blood shows also in the broad, fleshiness of Bryon's build, which at twenty and six years is already showing signs of running to fat. Testimony of his mother's blood is in a less fortunate manner. Barely tall enough to reach the shoulder of his younger brother, Bryon has inherited his mother's short stature. Combined with his fleshy build this gives him somewhat the appearance of a barrel.

The old man's now faded blue eyes touch upon each of his household present. Bryon and Griffon are each beloved by the old man, though his heart still aches at the loss of his two oldest sons. His daughter, Triona, is the very image of Connault's own mother, with hair the color of red gold and eyes so like the wild cornflowers. Delicate and slender, she is her father's treasure. At ten and six years, she should be wed, but the old man loved his daughter too much and had promised her a love match. Annu, wife of Bryon, is a mousey, silent girl of ten and nine. Though married to Bryon now for four years, she is only now to bear Connault's first grandchild. Father Adolphus, the Christian priest Bryon has brought to this house. A sometimes follower of the old ways, Connault cannot abide the man. He would shout him out of the room, but finds himself too weary to raise his voice, which takes on the petulant whine of a querulous old man.

"Why do you plague me so, priest? Get you out of my sight. I'll no have you mumbling an' murmuring o'er my death, you an' your impotent God, wringing your bony, scaled hands that whisper like a reptile's skin. Get you from my chamber, time enough when I am in that other place, to worry your beads an' mumble your prayers."

A deep obeisance is made and the old cleric draws back into the shadows. It is enough; at least Connault does not have to look upon the old crow in his dirty, black robes.

There stood his beloved Boann, given to him by her father, Brude, his liege Lord and king. She had been the youngest of Brude's daughters, and his favorite, though her birth did not come of the marriage bed. Her mother, Aguaine, was of the old Pictish race and a priestess of the Goddess, Danu. Brought here from the sacred isle of Iona, Aguaine had conceived Boann during the Beltaine festival and King Brude had taken the babe and her mother into his household. Though Boann had been an inexperienced girl when she was given to him, from the beginning she had asserted herself as a woman of royal Celtic blood. She was proud of her race and her tie to the old ones, confident of her ability to rule her house and her man. He respected her. Respect had grown into love; in all things Connault had consulted his Lady Wife, as he now would consult with her in his death. But first—

"I would tell you of my death an' how it was foretold to me. Yesterday noon, I went into the forest to visit the crofter, taking with me only my groom. Crofter had broken his leg in a fall ten days back an' I would see his woman and brood were cared for an' they would not want. I stayed overlong, dandling the youngest upon my knee an' enjoying Crofter's ale. Night was well along when I at last took my leave. I returned alone, having sent my groom on to his own bed long before. Well on my way to my own hearth, I came upon an old woman, wrapped in the widow's weed, perched on a stone wall, moaning and wailing her lament to the darkened sky. 'Old Grandmother, what do you here, an' who is it has passed?' I inquired of her, 'I ha' come to mourn the passing o' the auld Laird' came her reply to me. 'I fear you have been misled, an' moreover, are not from this land, else you would know it is I who is Lord of this country an' as you can see, I have not yet departed. From what land do you fare an' how come you to mourn one who is not dead?' Pointing off to the *sidhe*, the fairy mound, the old woman replied to me. 'I dwell there 'neath the gray rock mound. There I invite thee to join me. Soon shall we both be citizens of that country.' My horse shied and reared, the animal having a natural fear of things not of this world. Much effort it cost to control the beast and once I held the bit firm again, I looked back to the stone wall, and there saw naught of the old woman. In her place stood the hoodie crow, which picks at the bones that lay upon the battle field. It was Domnu, the death crone, and she has come for me. Even now, I hear the soft beating of her wings against the shuttered window. She has come to pluck the life from me, I feel the pull of my spirit as she seeks to snatch it from my breast."

"Rest easy, my Lord," said Bryon, "I have brought Father Adolphus here to pray for you. Christ will cast out the demon that has possessed you. You have only to give yourself up to Him and confess your sins before God and you shall be saved."

Connault's laughter at Bryon's most sincere declaration angered the priest, driving him silently from the chamber.

"Bryon, my son, if I were to confess my sins before this God of yours, my grandson, sitting there in my daughter-in-law's belly, would be awaiting the birth of his own son, before ever I was done. Go now all of you, I would be alone with my Lady."

As the brothers descended the mural stair within the castle wall, Griffon was deep in thought. A small smile escaped to play across his lips, though it did not reach his cold, gray eyes and was soon gone. His long stride carried him down the stone stair and into the Great Hall where he crossed quickly to the huge fireplace, where a great fire had been laid. Borne by stone corbels, a massive lintel stone formed the mantle. Bryon's short legs brought him scurrying after his younger brother. Their footfalls echoed hollowly against the stone walls which rose far over their heads. Huge rafters, also braced by stone corbels, supported the ceiling timber blackened by ages of oak and peat fires, throwing the sounds of their passage back into the near empty chamber. As he leaned against the cool stone, so thick and heavy it never seemed to completely absorb the fire's heat, with his fingers Griffon absently traced the intricately carved vine and leaf design which decorated the lintel. A habit learned in his youth and long ingrained, the touch of the complicated tracery seemed to give order to his thoughts. Bryon's nervous cough brought him back from reverie.

"Forgive me, brother, my mind was elsewhere."

"No small wonder, with talk of demons wandering the dark of night. Our father lying abed waiting for death to take him."

"More likely it is green ale that met our father on the road last night and holds him to his bed this morning. Crofter is not given to aging his ale overlong, brother. Our father, like every other mortal, will die, though I think not soon and surely not this night."

Again, the slightest of smiles touched Griffon's face. He loved his father very much and well knew of the old man's fondness for ale and a well-embroidered tale.

"Nay, Lord Griffon, not bad ale, nor this pagan banshee Domnu, my Lord Bryon." Father Adolphus moved silently from a shadowy corner. "A good Christian does not give in to these pagan beliefs, Lord Bryon." The old cleric shook a bony finger at the chastised young man, then warmed his hands before the roaring fire, for even in this temperate weather, the massive stone Keep had a damp chill, which would plague old bones.

"No, my young Lords, do not be taken in by talk of pagan demons and banshee that fill the stories of the peasants. There is a witch at work here, an evil sorceress who has cursed the old Lord to his death."

Bryon crossed himself almost without thought. Griffon, however, was not impressed and took no pains to hide his disbelief.

"Tell me, priest," he baited Adolphus, "how is it I would find this evil witch that I might do battle for the life of my father. I would meet this hag"

"You may laugh, Lord Griffon, but Christ has given me a vision of this mistress of the dark one who has cursed the old Lord. A hag she is not, my Lord. Her appearance is of a beautiful maid, so fair as to bring down the most pious of men. You must be on your guard. Her hair is black, black as the devil's seed and lips as red as blood. In form and dress, she is a wanton, that she might lure and tempt men to do her bidding; all the while she acts the innocent, for all appearances as pure as a chaste maiden. As to finding her, go to the place which is cursed by God, the sacred grove of the Druids, where the pagans perform their black rituals. Go to the well where the worship of the demon is carried out. There will you find her. She must be brought here to remove the curse and be purged of her sins."

"God, our Father in heaven," whispered Bryon, crossing himself again, "a vision, a miracle. Griffon, we must proceed with all haste to find this demon and bring her here before God."

Griffon stayed his brother with a hand upon his arm.

"I will go. If there is such a one, I will find her and bring her here. You are our father's heir and must remain here at his side."

He doubted much the priest's story, but he felt the need of an adventure and Griffon knew full well his brother was most definitely not the adventurous type.

One

Northern Ireland, Present Day

"Mrs. Ryan? You are Mrs. Judith Ryan, are you not?"

"Yes. Yes I am. I guess I'm just not used to being called that yet."

"Of course, you're a newlywed, aren't you? Well, welcome to Northern Ireland, Mrs. Ryan. May I call you Judith? I'm Colum Donnelly."

The man who extended his hand to Judith was Lord Colum Donnelly she realized. Tall and lanky, wearing the obligatory tweed of the gentry, he stood about five feet ten inches and would have been much taller but for a habit of bending slightly at the waist with his hands clasped behind his back. This odd habit gave him the appearance of a large tweed bird caught in the act of inspecting something at its feet. Taking his hand, Judith apologized for not recognizing him.

"Lord Donnelly, I'm so sorry I didn't recognize you. Peter has pictures of the two of you all over his... rather, our home. I guess I just didn't expect to see you here at the airport. I had expected Peter to meet me."

"Of course you would expect your husband to be here to meet you, and so he would have but for a last minute trip to Dun Tirlough to view the site."

Judith flipped her long black hair off her shoulder with an impatient gesture. Though, why she should be irritated she wasn't sure.

"Peter is at the castle then? Are we going to meet him there?"

After all, they had been married all of three days now, why should that lead her to believe he might be as anxious to see her as she was to see him? She couldn't help but remember how he had all but left her standing on the church steps in his haste to return to Northern Ireland.

"You can meet me there, once you've settled your affairs," he had told her when he handed her a ticket and left in a taxi for the airport.

"Why yes, we can stop at the castle if you like. Brilliant idea actually. Are these all your bags? You travel light, I see." Lord Donnally gestured to a dark suited man hovering at his elbow. The man collected Judith's few bags and quickly loaded them into the long, black automobile.

Soon they were traveling north from Belfast along the coast in Lord Donnelly's limousine.

"You must be fearfully tired, my dear. These flights can be brutal; California to New York, on to London then to Belfast. Dreadful trip, I should think."

"I am rather tired, your Lordship, though not too tired to admire this beautiful Irish countryside. You don't sound Irish, Lord Donnelly, are you?" Tact had never been Judith's long suit, and it seemed her curiosity always got the better of good judgment. But Lord Donnelly smiled at her indulgently.

"Colum, please. Your husband and I have been friends for years and I expect you and I to become fast friends as well. Actually, I do consider myself Irish; my people acquired Irish lands during the reign of Elizabeth the First. I was, of course, raised and schooled in England as my ancestors have always been.

"I think just a short stop at Dun Tirlough, then we'll have you off to the estate for a good rest before supper. I'm dreadfully sorry about spoiling your honeymoon, Judith. Peter and I have been trying for years to get permission for a dig at Dun Tirlough, then, out of nowhere, with no warning, the government relented and the permits came through. Unfortunately, that was just days before your wedding."

"To tell you the truth, Lord Donnelly... sorry, Colum, our wedding was just as spontaneous. Peter and I only met a short time ago. I had just completed my bachelor's degree at the University of California and was waiting to hear about being admitted to a master's program and just on a whim, I sat in on a lecture Peter was giving on the medieval architecture of Ireland. It was only later I realized he was the world's leading authority on the subject. He asked me to have coffee after the lecture. The rest happened so quickly, my head is still spinning."

"Good show, Peter. The old boy never seemed too keen on the fairer sex, although, I must say Peter seems to have brought home a first place winner his first time out."

Judith colored slightly at what Colum Donnelly seemed to think of as a compliment; at least, she thought he meant it to be a compliment. She was more than just a little uncomfortable with the squeeze Lord Donnelly gave her arm to emphasize his remark.

"How far is it to Dun Tirlough?" Flustered, she said the first thing to come into her head.

"It's still quite far my dear. Just sit back and enjoy the ride. Care for a drink?" Again, a physical emphasis went with the remark, this time a little pat on the knee.

A polite 'no' was all she could manage. It was all she could do to refrain from shrinking away to the far corner of the limo, and she did manage to beat back the look of disgust which kept trying to form on her face.

Judith knew that at twenty, she was considered a little naïve. Very naïve. She had mostly avoided men all of her relatively short adult life. She had entered the university at the tender age of sixteen and had known instinctively she would be a target for a certain type of man. Although Judith never really considered herself beautiful, she knew men were attracted to her. Her blue-black hair, against translucent white skin, coupled with brilliant green eyes, brought her a lot of male attention. She had always tried to avoid this kind attention and had managed to keep it in perspective. This man, however, made her very uncomfortable. Why couldn't Peter have just come to pick her up himself?

The limo moved quietly through the country. Typical of the Irish weather, the sky would alternate between black, heavy clouds, and brilliant sunlight. Judith's thoughts seemed to move in and out of shadow and light with the car.

When Peter began his courtship of her, Judith had been dazzled by the attention of a sophisticated older man. A world-renowned antiquarian. She had been swept along at a dizzying pace and when he had asked her to marry him... actually he hadn't asked her to marry him, he had just started referring to 'when they were married', assuming her consent. She had just followed along docilely.

The car sped along the coastal road, Judith's attention was drawn to the breathtaking scene being played before her eyes. Awesome cliffs ran down to the wild Irish Sea; bluffs of brilliant pastoral green were dotted with cattle and woolly sheep. Even the deep gloom of the leaden sky could not dull the magnificence of the Antrim Coast. The car slowed for the tiny villages they passed through, then sped up again, only to slow for the next, and the next.

The car burst suddenly into radiant sunlight and there stood Dun Tirlough, on the bluff below them. Her ruined walls like broken teeth against the gray sky. Her one standing tower a solitary guardian against the northern Irish coast; Scotland hovered like a thin blue-gray line on the far horizon. A strange feeling of *déjà vu* came over her, although she had never been to Northern Ireland before, or anywhere else for that matter. Perhaps, she had seen it in a photograph, she mused.

"What do you think of it, Judith?"

"She's beautiful." Judith said softly.

"Isn't it interesting you should refer to the castle as 'she'. Most people say 'it'." Colum Donnelly's voice droned on and on; an irritating buzz, which continually drew her attention from the fast approaching castle. Dun Tirlough.

"What does it mean, Dun Tirlough?"

"Nothing really. Dun is the Gaelic term for castle, or more properly, hill or ringed fort, which is how most of these castles began. Tirlough was probably an ancestral name. Perhaps the original landowner or clan leader."

"Dun Tirlough." She spoke the name softly, under her breath. The name conjured images of fierce warriors, clad in leather and coarse woolen, and women in richly embroidered gowns. Arthur and Guinevere—no wait, that was England, not Ireland.

As they approached the castle site, Judith could more readily see the extreme damage. Except for the one standing tower, there was very little that was recognizable as a building or dwelling. The ground was littered with tumbled down rock, which had once formed walls and buildings. What was left standing appeared as jagged puzzle pieces with gaping holes from which small trees and shrubs grew. Along the uneven tops of these ancient ramparts sprouted tufts of grass and wild flowers. As the car stopped, Peter appeared from behind one of those sections of still standing wall. Picking his way carefully through the tumble of building block stones strewn about, he made his way toward them. Forty years old, tall and rather wiry from years of fieldwork, with thinning blonde hair and rather watery brown eyes, Professor Peter Ryan was the very picture of the academic field researcher.

"Colum, I am so glad you decided to come here first instead of going directly to the estate. Oh, hello, my dear. So good to see you, pet. Colum, I've made the most marvelous find."

A brief brush of his lips against her cheek was meant as a greeting. At least he acknowledged her presence. Judith had noticed Peter often forgot she was present when he became involved with his colleagues.

Moving carefully through the half-buried rubble, Judith reached the partially standing section of wall Peter had been examining when they arrived. Running her hands along the ancient masonry as she moved alongside it she discovered the texture was much like any other stone wall. The stone felt cool when she pressed her face against the rough texture of the wall.

"What part of the castle is this?"

Both men turned in her direction. Peter, obviously irritated at being interrupted, Colum merely to see to which section she referred. It was Colum who answered.

"To be accurate, the section you refer to is not part of the Keep itself. The Keep is there by the cliff. That rectangular bit with the one complete tower and, though you can no longer see them, there were three more towers. That section there by you is part of the curtain wall, which protected the inner ward, where the family was housed. This area here where Peter and I are standing is the outer Bailey, which housed the fighting men, stables, armory and practice grounds, and was quite large. The outer curtain wall would have been way over in that direction and would have enclosed the entire area running from the cliff there around in a circular pattern to meet the cliff on the other side of the enclosure."

"What could possibly have happened to cause this much damage?"

Peter answered her. "Time, mainly, and neglect. This particular castle is extremely old; probably dating to the fifth or sixth century when the original hill fort was erected. Undoubtedly begun as a military outpost, this eventually was enlarged and fortified to house a family unit, the clan. At some point over the last ten or twelve centuries this location was abandoned. There is also the possibility of it having been destroyed by military action, possibly by Cromwell, though I doubt it. There isn't any record of Cromwellian activity in this particular region. There is evidence this particular Keep was very advanced in its defensive features. Five towers pierced the outer curtain wall, the men on the battlements could look down upon the enemy and drop any manner of deadly objects through the machicoulis. Then there was a heavily fortified inner wall. All in all, an extremely well protected fortress. No, I believe something occurred to prompt the abandonment of the site."

"Abandoned? Why would they?" She spoke more to herself than her two companions, neither of whom chose to answer her question, if they heard it at all.

"Well, Peter, unless you are ready to leave, I think I should take Judith on to the estate. A little rest after a long trip."

After another peck on the cheek, Peter handed Judith into the car and they again moved into the forest. She watched the castle grow smaller through the car window until it disappeared from sight, unable to tear her eyes from its retreating walls.

Two

Donnelly Estates, Northern Ireland

True to his word, Lord Donnelly had taken her directly from Dun Tirlough to the estate, where she and Peter would be staying in a lovely little stone cottage, which stood behind the manor house set in the middle of a lovely formal garden. A flagstone walk bordered by bright slashes of color from flowering annuals led up to a bright red, mock-Georgian front door. The brick and stone walls were covered with ivy, which grew right up to the gray slate roof. After Lord Donnelly left, Judith had fallen, exhausted, into bed, asleep even as her head touched the lovely hand embroidered pillowcase.

The soft patter of rain on the slate shingles of the roof pulled Judith back from a startlingly vivid dream. She had been...

...standing in the gloom of a primal forest. Lush, vibrant green ferns grew shoulder height beneath towering, closely growing conifers. The ground beneath her feet was carpeted with a thick layer of moss. Light

17

shone through the green canopy high over head, bathing everything with its pale glow. She was dressed in a fitted gown of fine wool, dyed to the darkest of dark blue. The sleeves were tight, like a second skin, but quite long and gathered at the wrist, half covering her hands. The gown was rounded at the neck and fell in soft voluminous folds across her breasts, though the bodice itself was so tight she could barely breath. At her hips, the gown flared ever so slightly, falling to the ground to pool at her feet. Over the gown, she wore an overtunic of very fine leather, open at the sides and belted with a girdle of beaten bronze and inlaid with gems. The neck and hem were richly embroidered with symbols she did not recognize. Around her neck, she wore a torq of heavy twisted gold, like thousands of strands of golden wire twisted together into a heavy rope. On her forehead had been painted a tattoo—a blue crescent— she could not see it, of course, but knew it was there.

Out of the forest gloom, came a large dark-haired man, leading an immense dark horse. The horse was all black but for long, silky-white, feathery hair growing from each knee down to its hooves. The animal was heavily muscled with a huge crested neck. Man and horse approached her. The size of the animal held her in awe, its back towering far above her own head. The man, as well, was of an immense stature and though she stared at both in wonder, she was not frightened of either. The man touched her cheek, gently, then lifted her to the horse's back. From a leather bag at his side, he removed a small parcel wrapped in pure white linen, which he offered to her, then placed in her hands. He looked up at her with an air of expectancy, as though he wanted, no, needed her to open the parcel. Inside, she found a living, still beating, heart. Rather than being frightened or repulsed, she found herself very moved by this gift. Carefully she rewrapped her precious parcel and cradled it gently in her lap. Seemingly satisfied by the care given to his gift, the man again took up the horse's reins, leading them into the forest from which he had come.

Startled again from sleep, her dream momentarily crowded coherent thought from her mind. She reached for Peter. *Peter! Where was he?* His side of the bed was untouched, not that Judith had any idea which side of the bed he preferred. Married for all of four days now and they had yet to spend a night together.

During their courtship, when Judith told Peter she was still a virgin, she had been pleased when he had told her he was in no hurry to begin a physical relationship. There would be plenty of time for that and he had seemed pleased she had waited for marriage.

Truthfully, her abstinence had very little to do with moral preferences or waiting for marriage. She simply had not found the right man. Still, she had accepted that he preferred to wait. However, when Peter had said there was no hurry, she had not realized he meant after they were married as well.

She found Peter in the breakfast room, already dressed and sipping his tea.

"Good morning, pet. Sleep well? Sorry I didn't wake you last night. Colum and I had much to discuss and you were sleeping so peacefully, I couldn't bear to wake you. Would you care for tea?"

"That's all right Peter. May I accompany you to the castle today? I promise I'll stay out of your way. Do you have coffee?"

"Yes, well, all right then. Perhaps you might be useful at that. Would you mind taking notes for me? The kettle's on the range, it will have to be instant if you want coffee."

"I would love to, thank you. Instant will be fine." Judith threw her arms around Peter's neck—kissing his cheek she then ran off to dress.

"No hurry, pet. Not much can be done until the rain quits us. What about your coffee?" he called after her.

~ * ~

Once the rains stopped, the day turned out to be glorious. The two men were deeply involved in their research leaving Judith to trail along behind them. She didn't mind, though. The sun was warm on her face and shoulders, the sea was spectacular, and Judith reveled in her own youth and vitality. She felt so alive and exhilarated, so ready to start this new life she and Peter were to share. There was some confusion, yes. Her desire to expand her own horizons, continue her education, battled with her desire for a family. Her own parents had died when she was very young and an aunt, an old spinster who'd had very little experience with children, had raised Judith. Because of this, Judith absolutely wanted a family of her own. She could have both, of this she was certain. Peter speaking abruptly to her interrupted her thoughts.

"Judith, pet, do try not to dawdle. I'm going to need you to take down some notes for me, there's a good girl." Suddenly, the day seemed not quite so glorious. Judith dragged her long black hair out of her face for about the umpteenth time and flung it over her shoulder, all the while trying desperately not to break an ankle on the rubble of the ruined castle that lay everywhere about them. Why did Peter always treat her in such a patronizing manner, as though she were a child? Had it been like this while he had courted her?

"Yes, Peter, I'm coming. My shoes are not really suited for this. I had not expected to be climbing around in this rubble. I thought this sort of work involved a lot of crouching over a small portion of dirt, flicking away at it with a brush."

"Really, Judith." Professor Ryan chided his young wife, "You were aware of the nature of my work, you did know we would be viewing the project site first. It must be carefully mapped and detailed before the work actually begins. How did you imagine we would accomplish anything without walking the site? Do please get your head out of the clouds and try to concentrate on the task at hand or better still, why don't you just wait for me in the car? There's a good girl."

Dismissed by her husband and thoroughly chastised, Judith felt her face turning crimson with embarrassment. She turned to leave, first making a hasty apology to Lord Donnelly.

As she picked her way back in the direction they had come, Judith felt the small hairs on the back of her arms rise. She was certain that Colum Donnelly was checking out her ass as she walked away. The man was a real perv.

"Colum, take note of this particular section here." Peter called to his friend.

"Yes, well..." With effort, Colum Donnelly wrenched his attention from Judith's retreating figure to focus on his friend and colleague. *She really does have a rather spectacular little bottom*, he thought to himself, *rather wasted on old Ryan*. He wondered idly if Ryan had managed to bed his young wife yet. He had been a friend of Peter Ryan's for over twenty-five years and this was the first time his friend had shown the slightest interest in a woman. Well, one never knows. Perhaps he might be of some service to the young bride after all. Laughing softly to himself, he gave his full attention back to Peter.

Stumbling through the rocky terrain and blinded by as yet unshed tears, Judith silently cursed herself for making Peter angry at her, berated herself for allowing Peter to chastise her like a small child. How had she wound up with such a cold, uncaring man? He hadn't been like this when they had first met. *Or had he?* Was she fooling herself, had she been so needy she had blinded herself to who he really was? Perhaps it was her fault. He'd been working so hard, and it was his honeymoon as well.

Judith caught scraps of their conversation as she moved cautiously through the fragments of castle wall scattered about the area. Quite unexpectedly, she unsettled a murder of ravens, which took to flight, noisily voicing their protest, then proceeding to wheel about overhead calling raucously to each other. Startled, Judith glanced up. Losing her footing, she tripped and fell to her hands and knees. *Blast and damnation,* she thought as she examined her hand. She had scraped it on a piece of stone jutting up from the grass. Looking closely, it appeared as though the stone had something carved on it. Brushing away the dirt and bits of loose grass clinging to it, Judith could clearly see there was something carved into the stone but couldn't make out what it was.

Finally, it all seemed just too much. She was supposed to be on her honeymoon. Her husband had confused her with his research assistant, having her following him around taking notes while crawling through the debris of a ruined castle, while this creepy old Lord something or other was copping a feel and staring at her ass every time she turned around. And now she had probably sprained her wrist. *Oh yes, we're definitely having fun now,* she thought to herself. The tears Judith had held back began to fall. This was all just too much. She swiped angrily at the tears when she heard the men returning, slipping the stone fragment into the pocket of her vest. She would not allow Peter the satisfaction of seeing her cry.

"There you are, Judith," Colum called out cheerfully. "Off we go back to the estate. I just know you're going to enjoy your stay in the cottage. I did promise you a tour of the grounds. I understand you're a botanist, Judith. So you must see the Druid groves. Of course, it isn't the original grove, which was destroyed by the early Christian priests during the seventh or eighth century. They burnt the trees to the ground and salted the earth as they seemed to think that would prevent anything from ever growing there again. I'm in the process now of having the grove replanted. Perhaps you could give me some advice?"

~ * ~

Later the same day, Colum presented himself at the cottage door, as promised. Peter was entirely too absorbed in his notes. And not particularly interested in the local flora, he declined the invitation to join them on their tour. This didn't seem to bother Lord Donnelly in the least. Judith, however, was anxious to get out of the cottage. She had tried several times to involve Peter in discussion about their future. She had wanted to talk about the things about which every new couple was concerned. Children, for example. Judith wanted children, lots of them. And Peter wasn't exactly a young man. Then there was her education, she felt she was young and strong enough to have children and a career. He had finally shut himself in the study.

Granted, these were things they should have discussed before marriage, but everything had happened so quickly. Well, she wanted to talk about them now. But he would not discuss these or any other issues with her. He wouldn't even listen to her. Then there was this sex thing. Before they were married, okay, she could see wanting to wait, but now they were married he seemed no more interested in her than before.

"Judith... Judith?" She became aware that Colum was talking to her, and had been, in fact, for some time. They had walked deep into a large grove of trees—yews, rowan, willow, and a particularly spectacular copper beech, all traditionally endowed with spiritual powers by the Druids. This was what he had been speaking of earlier. His hand on her arm raised the hairs on the back of her neck and she moved away from the touch. He seemed not to notice.

"Over here, you will find the single most important feature of these groves, an authentic Druid well. The same priests who had destroyed the grove had, of course, destroyed the well. We located the well and as you can see, the stones have all been found and replaced, except for those from this front portion. Careful, the stones are loose; they haven't been mortared as yet. The original did not use mortar but for the sake of safety, we will. The well itself is being excavated. We have removed dirt and rock down approximately forty feet and we have just unearthed our first major recovery." He reached into his pocket and presented Judith with a small circular object.

"It's a ring, a man's ring judging from the size and the figure inlayed on it. Although it's badly eroded and one is unable to tell by looking at it, the ring is fashioned from silver with an inlay of coral and jade. The figure is of a mythological beast, part lion, and part eagle. See there is the lion's head and the wings are just there. Quite clever, really—exquisite workmanship, don't you think? Probably sixth or seventh century."

Looking closely at the ring, Judith recognized the figure, which Colum was describing, was the same as the figure etched on the bit of stone she had found earlier that day.

Taking the stone from her pocket, Judith held it out to Lord Donnelly.

"It's the same as this. The figure I mean. Isn't it? Do you suppose the ring belonged to the same person who carved this bit of stone? I found it back at Dun Tirlough." Judith suddenly realized she probably shouldn't have removed the stone from the site; it might be an important discovery. "I guess I shouldn't have picked it up," she apologized.

Examining the stone carefully, Lord Donnelly shook his head slowly. "Highly unlikely, I should think. We are talking about over forty kilometers between the two sites. In that day, quite a distance. Besides, the gryphon was a common Celtic symbol during that era, all through the Dark Ages, in fact. It is possible, of course, but not likely. And I wouldn't worry about taking it from the site. Let Peter know where you found it so he can log it in."

"How did the ring come to be in the well, do you think?" Musing softly to herself, she turned the ring repeatedly, examining it closely. Something about this ring seemed familiar, as though she had seen it before, probably due to the similarity between the two figures.

"The ancient Celts were pagans. They worshipped a pantheon of Gods and Goddesses. These deities served many purposes for the ancients—war, famine, marriage, the birth of a child, all of these were major events or needs in one's life. To ensure the outcome you desired, you had to appease the one God or Goddess who was associated with an event or need. The pagans believed these deities lived in an underworld, the entrance to which was referred to as a sidhe, pronounced 'shee', or fairy mound, a small rounded hillock. We now know passage tombs were the ritual burial places of the original people of Ireland. They were indeed very sacred places to the people who built them, just not for the same reason as for the Celts. The Druids believed gifts of riches, such as jewelry, gold and silver plates, bowls, chalices, as well as arms, should be offered up to their Gods and Goddesses in return for various favors—relief from famine, drought, plague or the making of a good marriage, a birth, anything which seemed out of the control of mortal man. What better way to deliver up these offerings, without actually entering this underworld, but by tossing them down a well? And so, there was a network of these sacred groves and wells throughout the British Isles and most likely, the continent. Of course, most of the truly valuable pieces were recovered from these wells prior to their being filled in. Those early Christian priests may have been fanatics, but they weren't stupid. Some believe this ancient Druid practice was actually the forerunner of our modern day tradition of tossing coins into a well and making a wish."

"How intriguing. What a remarkable story. It's so romantic, don't you think?"

"Romantic? Yes, well I suppose a young woman might find the thought of Druid rituals and seventh century Celtic warriors quite romantic. Rather like those romance novels you girls like, yes?"

Lord Donnelly had drawn rather close, both her hands clasped in his rather sweaty ones.

Judith tried to back away, but Lord Donnelly held on to her hands, pressing them tightly against his chest. Then, seeming to realize her discomfort, he released her and continued as though nothing untoward had occurred.

"I'm not so sure, though, Judith. With your black hair and being of such a small stature, you could very well have been thought to have the ancient blood, one of the fairy people, not very popular with the Christians of that time. Women in general were not highly thought of, my dear. Not much more than breeders, married for their clan name and the children they would produce. A woman's family line was more important than anything else."

Leaning over the edge of the well, Judith could almost picture herself a thousand years ago—a very different Judith in manner and dress, a different world a thousand years or more in the past, leaning over the edge of the well on this very spot. Wishing fervently for her heart's desire, she would have thrown some precious article into the well. The picture seemed so real, she could almost feel the touch of a fine woolen garment against her skin. Why not? Judith had never been particularly religious and had always found praying to her own God rather unsatisfying. Perhaps praying to the Gods and Goddesses of another era would fill some need within her. All Gods were really the same God, weren't they? Different names for the same concept. Could it possibly matter by what name you called him... or her?

"Over here Judith, you'll find a particularly lovely old hawthorn." Lost in her own thoughts, Judith allowed herself to be guided through the grove. His Lordship chattered on, giving Judith's elbow the occasional squeeze. She would nod at the appropriate moments so as not to offend, though she wasn't really listening.

The Dark Ages. The very words conjured images of Druid kings and warrior knights who pledged devotion to their ladies. *Oh yes, an era where men were men and women were merely a commodity*, she thought, mentally taking herself in hand. She was having enough trouble handling one man in the here and now. What on earth would she do with a whole world full of men who considered her nothing more than a breeder, a piece of property at best. But were those men of that era significantly different than the men of today? They still seemed to think of women as property.

"The one I have now treats me like a piece of furniture, what's so different?" she wondered, half out loud.

"I beg your pardon, you were saying?"

"Nothing, Colum, just thinking out loud. Now, what were you saying about this wonderful old oak?"

Colum droned on and on.

Later the same evening, Judith returned alone to the Druid well, drawn by some unknown need. She wandered among the trees. The sun, just beginning to set, washed the grove with crimson. She could smell the sea in the mist, rising with the approach of evening. Though the ocean and Dun Tirlough were thirty miles away, she could taste the salt in the air and brought the castle easily to mind as it must have been in all of its glory. It was quiet here; the deep shadows and cool moss invited one to sit. She laid her cheek against the cool stone of the old well, thinking back to her earlier conversation with Lord Donnelly, and about Danu the Mother Goddess.

"Where did I go wrong? Danu, where did I lose my way? Are you really out there somewhere?" Immediately feeling foolish, Judith pulled herself together and returned to the cottage. She had made her own bed, as the saying goes, now she would have to see to it that it was fit to lie in.

That night, Judith stood at the large cottage window looking out over the formal gardens and beyond to the Druid groves, then further still to a low range of hills. Dun Tirlough was somewhere on the other side of those mountains. A mist crept silently over and through the peaks and glens of the low mountain range, seeking the low ground; an eerie sight. A storm was brewing. In the last of the evening light she could see it building over the low Irish mountains. Towering black clouds stacked up behind some invisible atmospheric barrier. Small flashes of lightening from within the massive cloudbank flared briefly, momentarily lighting a narrow patch of black and illuminating the hills. Soon, whatever barrier of nature that held the storm at bay would collapse, loosing the fury. Judith hugged her thin negligee to her. Somehow, she had to get through to Peter. Turning her back to the window and the approaching storm, Judith faced the storm just beginning to rage within the small cottage.

"I don't understand you, Peter. Don't you want children, to have a family? Your supposed friend, Colum Donnelly, seems to display more of an interest in me than you do."

"Very well, Judith, since you insist on discussing this, no, I do not want children. Children are a distraction and only disrupt a household. Messy little creatures. And further more, I will not have you spewing out your childish female delusions about a friend and staunch supporter of my work. Your little attempt at rousing my jealousy is infantile and useless. Nor will you be returning to the university. I have a very full social life. I entertain my colleagues regularly and I expect the management of my house to be your primary concern."

"For the love of God, Peter, do you hear yourself? Your social life, your colleagues, your house! You don't need a wife; you need a housekeeper and a social secretary. Peter, I want children, and I would like to continue my education, I want a career someday. I'm young and strong, I can do all of those things and still maintain a home."

"A career! Judith, you play with plants, what kind of career is that? I married you because you are reasonably attractive and will be a satisfactory addition to my life and my career. I needed someone reasonably competent to manage my home. The fact that you are a woman with some limited intelligence, which I can put to use in my research, is of course, an added bonus. You should be grateful I rescued you from the world of academia for which women are so obviously ill-suited."

"You are the most pompous, arrogant..." The crack of Peter's hand across her cheek cut short Judith's words, and she stumbled back against the wall. Stunned, Judith stared at her husband in disbelief. His face held no expression whatsoever, not anger, not anything. Her hand gently held the place where the imprint of Peter's hand was already starting to swell her cheek.

"Now, listen to me very carefully, pet. We will not discuss this again. I will not tolerate another outburst like the one I just witnessed. You will never use that tone or raise your voice to me again."

He sounded so reasonable, so... rational, as though he was speaking to a disobedient child. Judith edged away as he advanced on her.

"I will overlook it this time, however, if you question me just one more time, I will be forced to punish you."

"You are insane," she whispered, still holding her throbbing face. "I'm leaving, Peter. Don't try to stop me."

Before she could slip past him, Peter struck her again, knocking her to the floor. As before, his face was calm, his manner composed. He might be lecturing before a room full of students for all the emotion he displayed.

"Look what you made me do. I told you I would have to punish you if you did not show me the proper respect. You will learn to always speak to me with respect. Never will you speak to me in that manner again. The trouble with women today is they have not been taught to give proper respect to their husbands. They have been allowed to speak their minds without being disciplined. You will learn discipline, Judith."

Peter loosened his belt as he stood over her.

"I thought I had found a perfect, obedient little lady in you, Judith. My pretty little virgin. But, I was wrong. All I hear from you is sex, sex, sex. You want sex, Judith? Very well, you shall have it."

Judith tried to desperately to scramble away from Peter but found herself trapped beneath his weight. He straddled her legs, shoving her thin gown up above her waist. She struggled against him, raking his face with her fingernails. Peter struck her again, then seized her by the throat with one powerful hand, cutting off her breath. If she did not do something quickly she would lose consciousness; perhaps she would die. She was certain Peter intended to rape her. As her vision began to gray around the edges, Judith brought the heel of her hand up hard, smashing the bridge of his nose. He roared in pain and clutched his bleeding nose with both hands, allowing Judith to suck in much needed air. Her vision began to clear, but she was not out of danger yet. Peter still sat on her legs and she was not strong enough to forcibly remove him. Without thinking, she reached out, grabbed him by the testicles, and twisted. He rolled away from her, releasing her legs and howling with pain and rage.

Gagging and retching, Peter writhed on the floor. Clutching at his groin he managed to gasp, "I'll kill you, slut. Judith! Where do you think you are going? Come back here, bitch."

Peter's screams of rage followed her out of the cottage as Judith threw open the door and fled into the approaching storm. Through the garden and into the sheltering trees of the Druid grove, she ran. Past the hawthorn and the rowans and oaks. She ran. The wind wailed through the treetops, which thrashed and raged in reply. Deep groans came from their straining trunks. The rain would come soon and still Judith ran.

~ * ~

She knew exactly were she was headed. It seemed she had been headed there since she had arrived on this island. She heard Peter behind her. Fear clutched at her burning throat increasing the pain from Peter's abuse. Her heart fluttered like a small, frightened bird, beating itself against its cage.

The well was just ahead. She touched her bruised throat gingerly, her fingers encountering the twisted gold chain there, a distinctive red-gold antique piece, the only thing she owned that had been her mother's. She had reached the well, now there was nowhere to go. Peter was behind her and he was insane, she knew it as certainly as she knew her own name. Tearing the chain from her neck, Judith leaned far out over the well.

"Danu, Mother Goddess, somehow I know you are out there... I pray you are really here. There is very little in this life I really want. I want to love a man who will love and respect me in return. Do I ask for too much? Oh, Mother, please help me. Help me!"

As the chain slipped from her fingers, she watched it fall. The loose stones gave way under her weight. The screaming of the storm raged all around her. She didn't fight the fall. She surrendered to it—just let herself slip away, following the chain into the darkness of the well.

Three

Sacred Druid Grove, 678 AD

Griffon sat with an elbow resting on his knee, propped against the lichen-covered stones of the Druid well. An early morning mist crept through the dense undergrowth bringing with it the pungent odors of the conifer forest. The morning chill still clung to the air. Weak streaks of a pale dawn tried in vain to penetrate the dense canopy of the forest. Heavy black clouds seemed to hang just out of reach of the towering treetops. It would rain soon. His gaze strayed, not for the first time, back to the woman. He had found her here in the early dawn hours, at the very spot of which Adolphus had spoken.

She lay upon a bed of moss at the foot of the Druid well. To find a woman alone in this wild, remote place, a place of secrets and rituals, should have seemed uncommon strange. But Griffon found it pleased him immensely. Though he could not say why he found it so. A small break in the clouds sent a shaft of brilliant sunlight down to play among the trees. Griffon watched small rainbows form in the mist rising from the forest floor. A sigh again brought his attention back to the woman. Sleep did not appear to comfort her because twice she had cried out softly, one small white hand raised vaguely to ward off some unseen blow.

He considered again the angry red imprint of a man's hand, which marred the perfect white skin of her cheek. He had known men who felt the need to use their hands on their women in such a manner, though he could see no honor in the use of such violence against one so small and fragile. The other cheek lay pillowed upon the upturned palm of one small hand; a thin gold band encircled the ring finger. What manner of man would leave his woman unprotected in these wild forests? Perhaps she had ventured here on her own, seeking the protection of the gods who inhabited this place. Could this possibly be the one for whom the old priest sent him to search?

She was no bigger than a small boy of ten and two years, although the thin lace gown she wore, damp and clinging to softly rounded curves, left little doubt this was no child and definitely no boy. A broad smile spread across his face at the reaction this creature brought to his body. He sat at the foot of the well, content to watch her sleep—for now; the soft rise and fall of her breast with each breath, listening to the small sighs and murmurs, which escaped from her dreams. Breaking through the clouds, sunlight touched the raven-black hair spread fanlike about her shoulders and head, there turning to blue fire. Her eyes opened, sightless in sleep, to reveal startling green, then drooped to close again. He would waken her, so she might turn those emerald lamps upon him.

"Truly, Lady, do you sleep still? I have waited long for you to awaken."

At the sound of his voice in the still forest morning, the woman's eyes flew open, wild and startled. She tensed as though ready to leap and run at the slightest untoward movement. She settled those large, frightened eyes upon him and his breath caught as though an unseen hand had closed about his throat. Instinctively, she moved to distance herself from him. Griffon moved more quickly. Capturing his prize by one small ankle, he pulled her back, and again he smiled. This time at the way her gown rode up about her thighs as she fought to maintain her modesty.

"Do you leave so soon, Lady? Would you have me think my company does not please you? I apologize for in truth, I fear I must have startled you."

The woman's fear did not seem directed at Griffon though she continued to try to extricate her ankle from his grasp. She seemed distracted, nervous. Her eyes strayed continually to the forest around her, seeking some hidden danger behind each tree.

"Let me go. I must leave this place." Her words were small and frightened. Her eyes did not touch him, but continued to search the shadows. It frustrated him that she did not look directly at him; she did not truly see him. She hugged her arms across her chest, an instinctive gesture of self-protection. Again, she pulled against his iron grip, which held her trapped like a small rabbit caught in the hunter's snare. Or was it he who was falling into her snare? The old cleric had said she would tempt and lure him to her bidding.

"Sit you still," He commanded, giving the captive ankle a sharp tug. "I would consider a moment... fair of face, so fair as to bring down the most pious of men... just so, as beautiful as any I have every seen. Hair as black as the devil's seed. Aye, but small evidence in itself as I also carry that testimony upon my own head... and blood red lips that pout prettily. All and all, a tempting feast to find spread upon the forest floor waiting to be sampled. Yes, and see how she does strive to hide her nakedness, as any chaste maiden would. And haven't I found this banquet but at the very spot, which was foretold to me? Aye, the priest spoke well. What say you, Lady, have I found my witch?"

At that, the woman turned her full attention to him. She seemed to really look at him for the first time. Suddenly aware of the woman's scrutiny, Griffon tugged at his unruly, black hair. As usual, it had pulled free from the leather thong that held it in place and he attempted to bring it back into some kind of control. He was not wearing his usual traveling garb. In the event the priest had been accurate in his vision of a malevolent sorceress, Griffon had made sure to wear a very special leather armband. It had been worked over with magical incantations and had been a gift from his mother to protect him in battle. He touched briefly the torq he wore about his neck—his favorite, the one that had been a gift from his grandsire in the last tournament at the king's court. He brushed energetically at the dust and random bits of debris that clung to his leather tunic. There was naught he could do about the mud that covered his boots, which were of a soft split leather, held together with leather strapping, which bound them tightly to powerful calves.

She frowned slightly then shook her head impatiently. "You don't understand, I have to get away from here, I must leave this place now. He will be looking for me. He's insane." this last spoken at no more than a whisper, as though she spoke only to herself.

Leaning close, Griffon took her chin in his hand, holding her tightly as she tried to pull away from his grasp. Lifting and tilting her face from side to side, he examined closely the bruises on her face and neck.

"It's badly used you've been, my Lady."

"Please, let me go. I can't let him find me." Tears welled up in her eyes and threatened to spill.

"Sadly, I cannot."

Looking deeply into brilliant green eyes where tears spilled over to slide slowly down her cheeks, Griffon sought to reassure her. Her tears slid down his thumb, which held her chin, to pool in the palm of his hand like so many tiny diamonds.

"You have no need to fear, Lady." Too late, he noticed her arm swing round. Perhaps he was distracted by the feel of satiny white skin beneath his callused hand or by the barest blush of rose upon a translucent white cheek. Whatever the cause, Griffon was caught off guard as the woman swung wildly, her fear lending strength, catching him on the left temple with a small jagged rock. She dropped the rock and stumbled to her feet, running.

Griffon shook off the blow and ran after her. He caught her easily and slung her over his shoulder. Unwilling to risk harming the woman in order to subdue her, Griffon was unsure what to do with this wild demon he had captured. Her small fists rained ineffectual blows against his broad back, and she kicked wildly, as she screamed for help at the top of her lungs. By his account, it was not she who was in need of help just now. Impatient and frustrated, Griffon bellowed a command for silence.

Startled by the command, and the power with which it was given, the woman fell still and silent. Griffon placed her upon her feet.

"We'll have no more of this, yes? You will be silent and behave or won't I be forced to bind you hand and foot, and toss you across the back of my horse?"

They were both covered with blood... his. Griffon ran his hand across his face, discovering much blood, but little damage.

"I congratulate you, my Lady, I have not often been bloodied in battle, and never by one so small—or fierce. Perhaps I should have worn armor into this battle."

The woman seemed appalled by all the blood; nervous and confused but no longer hysterical.

"I am so sorry. I was frightened; I lost control just for the moment. I didn't mean to... I really must leave this place. My husband..."

She reached out to touch his bloody face, but hesitated and withdrew her hand.

"Why are you doing this to me? What do you want?"

"First, I would have you cover yourself," He said, taking his red wool mantle from his script and draping it about her shoulders. He had to bend low over her small height to fasten the bronze brooch at her shoulder. *Roses, her hair smelled of roses.* An irrelevant thought to occur at this moment, he pushed it to the back of his mind.

"While I have truly enjoyed your present state of undress, my Lady, in such close proximity, isn't it more than a man can be expected to bear without acting upon his natural inclinations?"

Blushing furiously, she suddenly found the ground at her feet in need of inspection. A shining black wing of hair hid her face.

"Why do you call me 'Lady' as though it were a title? My name is Judith."

Grinning broadly at her obvious attempt to change the subject, Griffon replied, "And how would I have addressed you, knowing not by what you were called?"

"Then you didn't know my name? My husband didn't send you looking for me, to take me back?" Her gaze searched his face as though she might find the truth written there.

So that was the way of it. She had run from her husband, most likely for the reasons so clearly marked upon her face. She feared he had been sent to fetch her back to this abusive master.

"Sit yourself down, Lady Judith. You need have no fear that I am sent to fetch you back to your husband. Haven't I been sent by the priest, Father Adolphus, who would have me deliver you to Dun Tirlough?"

"Father Adolphus? A priest has sent for me?" Perhaps Colum Donnelly had asked the priest to intercede.

"Aye, so it is."

Her relief was visible; hardly the expected reaction of a witch. Then it had been the husband she feared.

"Since you are to be my rescuer, may I know your name?"

Rescuer? Perhaps not, he thought with no small regret.

"A fair question, Lady Judith. I am called Griffon mac Connault, youngest son of Connault of Dun Tirlough. Liege man of my Lord Brennus, who is sovereign of this country and brother to my Lady Mother."

"Something which you said before, you were looking for a witch. I don't understand."

Now it was Griffon's turn to change the subject. He did not wish to further agitate her, especially now she felt somewhat safe in his company.

"We'll leave that for later, won't we? For now, we must quit this place. The Druids do not welcome intrusion into their sacred places and guard them jealously. Haven't your cries alerted those who watch over this place already?"

Griffon noted Judith's puzzled look as he spoke, but thought little of it. She seemed to become anxious as she realized he could be correct. Someone may have heard her cries. But who; the husband, perhaps? She did not question him further, though he did notice she seemed to regard their surroundings anew. The lady remained quite docile as he placed her upon Lugh's broad back. The huge Shire horse would not even notice the addition of her slight weight. Griffon mounted and settled Judith within the protective circle of his arms. There she would be unable to attempt an escape, rather than behind where she might slip to the ground and run. Well, that's what he admitted to himself, isn't it? She looked back only once. Placing both her hands on his arm, she leaned out in order that she might peer around him. Again, she looked at him in a questioning manner but said nothing.

Long after she had settled back, Griffon could still feel the warmth of her touch on the bare flesh of his arm. At first, she held herself stiff and away from him; though, as they distanced themselves from the Druid grove, the woman seemed to relax. It began to rain and although she would remain dry within the cocoon of his wool mantle, she burrowed against him to get way from the sudden downpour. As was the way in his country, the rain quit them as quickly as it came, leaving in its stead the heat of the Irish sun.

Griffon reveled in the warmth of the sun on his bare skin, the feel of Lugh's gait and the woman in his arms who rocked gently with it. The smell of her near drove him to distraction — roses, and the musky scent of a woman.

In time, she slept. Lifting the mantle hood away from her face, Griffon captured a long, heavy lock of raven hair and touched it to his cheek. The scent of roses grew stronger. Her head rocked back against his shoulder and he was again confronted with the evidence of abuse the woman wore upon her face and neck. Rage darkened his emotions—though why he should care what some unknown man did with his wife, he did not know and did not care. If Judith had awakened at that moment, she would have been met with the countenance, which had won Griffon his name as a warrior to be feared, even at his young age. Would he had this abuser before him now, perhaps he would make Lady Judith a widow.

Four

Judith awoke to the smell of wet wool and the warmth of that small bit of sun that managed to work its way through the thick forest growth. She found herself snuggled against Griffon's muscular, unyielding chest. He had one arm about her waist, holding her tightly against him. So she would not slip off as she slept? She found the sensation comforting and... familiar?

With the other hand he guided Lugh. Griffon had introduced her to Lugh back at the well. Named for the Druid deity, Lugh of the Long Arms, she had laughed with delight at the name in spite of her circumstances. The great Shire horse was aptly named, being an exceptionally large animal with very, very long legs. Griffon had explained to her that the animals were bred for their stature and strength because of the need to carry a man into battle in full armor as well as the heavy weapons of war. Moreover, Judith had immediately recognized the horse, then Griffon, as the mysterious dark-haired man and horse from her dream the night before.

Judith feigned sleep that she might have time to think. When Griffon had awakened her earlier, at the well, she had been deep in a troubled dream—fighting off a nightmarish Peter, a grotesque slavering monster who chased her through the tangled maze of perfectly clipped hedges of a formal English garden, a garden which somehow gave the feeling of intense evil. The sound of Griffon's voice had pulled her from that dream, though the vision, the terror of it, had stayed with her. Still caught in that nightmare world, she had been badly frightened, and reacted with near hysteria. She had just wanted to get away, though she had never felt any fear of the dark-haired man. Perhaps, subconsciously, she had already associated him with the more pleasant dream of the previous night.

The first impression she had of Griffon was of massive size, tall, with broad shoulders and muscular arms and chest. Now she took a closer look. His hands were large, and coarsened by hard work. Looking up at him, she noticed the long black hair, which curled about his face in the damp morning air, tied back with a leather thong. Truant sable curls clung damply about his face and neck, escaped their leather binding and played about his face. Dark gray eyes stared off in the distance, beyond the trees and undergrowth of the forest at... what? The muscular arms, bare, except for a wide leather band which encircled his upper arm. The band was covered with embroidered symbols and magical incantations. Her gaze lingered there. They seemed somehow familiar, as though she should know what they meant. A heavy gold arm ring displaying a mantling bird, perched upon the head of a Goddess on each terminal, banded the other arm. A soft deerskin tunic covered his broad chest and a heavy twisted gold torq encircled his neck. The tunic was richly embroidered in patterns of intertwined lines forming intricate knots, ornamentation of silver worked into each side

"You're awake, then. It's time to stop. You have yet to break your fast and we have much of which we must speak."

Suddenly reluctant to leave her protected nest, Judith did not want to explore the implications of what had happened that morning and made no move to leave the horse's back. Her reluctance seemed to go unnoticed, for Griffon did not seem to expect her to move, he simply swept her up, and slid from Lugh's back with her held tightly in his arms. The sudden drop from that great height caused her to gasp and throw her arms about his neck.

Laughing, Griffon placed her upon her feet. She very much liked the sound of his laughter.

Not for the first time, she realized how ludicrous this whole situation was. She had allowed herself to be carried off by a very imposing man, into what appeared to be an extremely remote wilderness, with little idea of where he was taking her or of his intentions toward her. Of course, if his intentions had been rape or murder, he could have easily accomplished that back at the well. Judith had always relied upon her instincts about people, and all of her instincts told her this man would not harm her. But then, look at how badly she had misjudged Peter.

The spot Griffon had chosen to stop immediately charmed Judith. Taking her hand in an archaic and courtly manner, Griffon led her to a low, sunny spot on a shelf of stone, which overhung a swiftly moving stream. Close growing trees formed a lacy canopy over the rushing torrent. Judith dipped her feet into the racing water as it pounded down out of the mountains, tumbling over rocks and ledges in its hurry to descend from the mountainside. Flashes of silver caught her eye and she leaned over to catch a closer glimpse of the tiny darting fish, riding the rapids to what lay ahead.

"Careful, little one. If you should tumble into the water I would be hard pressed to find what would be left of you."

Griffon handed her a piece of soft bread and some hard cheese, then sprawled on the grass beside her stony perch. Nibbling at the bread, Judith decided to see what she could learn from Griffon.

"You said we were going to Dun Tirlough. Is there a village near the castle? Is that where the priest is? Why would this Father Adolphus send for me? Does he know my husband?"

"Hold woman," he exclaimed, laughing. "I can not think swiftly enough to answer these many questions you hurl at my head. Aye, our destination is Dun Tirlough, which is my home. There is no village, only the castle. All who are retainers there live within the castle walls, except those who tend the fields, the forest, or the cattle. They each live within their own stone rath. I am sent to fetch you, or rather someone I would find there in the spot where I found you, to answer to Adolphus, who has called you witch. This Adolphus is a Christian, and sees demons and witches in every shadow. The people of my Lady Mother have a deeper knowledge of such things and do not so easily quake at shadows in the dark."

Judith sat as still as stone, like a lamp slowly turned up to light a room, the realization of what he was saying alighted in her mind. He had mentioned a witch earlier, at the well. She had heard, but it had not registered. Was the man insane? She almost laughed. Two mad men in as many days, what were the odds?

"What are you saying? Are you telling me I have somehow been transported to ancient Ireland and I am accused of sorcery, witchcraft?"

"I know naught of this place you call Ireland. This country is of the Ulaid, called Ulster, and is ruled by Brennus. Aye, it is ancient, the tribes of the Celts have long held this land, and the old ones before. As to sorcery, it's not I which accuse. I have been sent to fetch a woman who was told to me by one who might have studied your likeness only moments before telling it to me. I was charged to find this woman at the very place where I did find you. It is not for me to say if you are she whom Adolphus seeks, only to bring you to Dun Tirlough. Now eat, I would travel further before this day is gone."

Ancient Ireland—the Dark Ages—where pagan beliefs mingled freely with Christian doctrine. Judith's thoughts went back to the previous night and Peter's sudden and unexpected descent into madness. Running through that terrifying storm into the Druid grove. The storm tearing at her and Peter fast on her heels. She recalled finding herself at the well and throwing her prayers into the inky, black depths, the offering of her gold chain, and herself as well, only to awaken in a world changed.

And there was no denying it, that place had changed. In the clearing by the well, nothing was as it had been the day before. The trees had been different, and she was a botanist after all. She knew about those things. Yesterday, the area around the well had held hawthorn, oak, and rowan. This morning that same area was no longer the cultivated garden-like forest she remembered. This morning it had been wild, remote, untamed and, yes, it still held hawthorn and oak and rowan, but it was not the same. Now it also held conifers, tall, virgin trees, and a low growing tangle of undergrowth found only in an ancient, untouched, forest.

And this track they had been traveling was hardly more than a deer trail. They hadn't encountered a single soul all day. This was definitely not the same forest she and Colum Donnelly had driven through yesterday. Even the air smelled different, cleaner... no smog.

And this man, look how he dressed and spoke.

"It can't be. This cannot be where or when you say this is." Turning to Griffon, she asked, "What year is this? Please I must know."

"It is the seventh year of the rule of Brennus, son of Brude. Though the Christians name it differently, calling it the six hundred and seventy eighth year of the God they call Jehovah."

Judith clamped both hands across her mouth to stifle the cry, which rose in her throat. Perhaps it was she who was insane. And yet, there may be an explanation. Perhaps she was right now, at this moment, lying at the bottom of the well or in a hospital bed, and this was just a dream brought on by delirium or drugs. Yes, she was dreaming and the dream would soon end. Satisfied with her explanation Judith relaxed visibly. Best just to let things proceed. After all, it was not an unpleasant dream.

"It matters not what can or cannot be, only what is..." Griffon's reply was cut short, he held his hand up for silence, his attention diverted by the sound of a horse approaching. Drawing his broadsword and taking Judith by the arm, Griffon moved swiftly toward the trees.

"Do as I say, do not argue," he whispered quietly into her ear. "Make no sound." He thrust her into an embrasure formed by small trees grown close together. His back to her, Griffon placed himself between Judith and those who advanced upon them. Feet firmly planted, broadsword in hand, Griffon prepared to defend the lady whom he had met only hours earlier. Judith peeked out from around Griffon's legs at the encroaching danger.

Three men approached. Two rode double while the third walked beside the horse; if one could call the rude collection of bone held together by a loose skin covering forming a gross caricature of a horse. The two who rode its back would have traveled more quickly had they carried the beast upon their own backs.

Griffon knew these men had seen him, his sword drawn—ready to do battle. What was more important, he knew that Judith had been seen as well—her small, frightened face peeking out from the dark behind him. These men knew it was a woman he protected. What else would a man guard so jealously? What wealth a man carried was easily concealed on his person and it would be obvious to even these loathsome creatures that Griffon was born to fight on horse or foot. But to stand his guard upon a coppice of trees could only mean a woman or a small child. Either would be vulnerable in a fight on horseback or in the open. To men such as these there would be little opportunity to even look upon a noble woman, let alone come close enough to touch her. Any woman these creatures were likely to enjoy, would be the coarse, wrung out women who offered themselves for purchase at the local taverns or markets.

These men were in no better condition than the horse they rode; thin and gaunt, eyes hollow and feverish, they nevertheless approached upon Griffon steadily. Instinct told Griffon they would split and approach him from three sides. As expected, they did just that, picking up any weapons they could find as they approached—tree limbs that could be used as clubs, as well as rocks, would have to do for these were wretched, poor men unlikely to have a blade between them. Steadily they approached, dividing Griffon's attention between them. Griffon's sword flashed silver in the sun as he swung it in slow sweeping arches. Crouching low on powerful legs, he prepared himself. The tall, thin one on his left swallowed nervously, passing a hand over feverish eyes. The smaller one on his right had a crooked leg, which he dragged behind him. The middle one flinched and ticked with some nervous affliction while jabbering softly to himself, flecks of white foam at the corners of his mouth. Griffon heard the sound of Judith forcing herself further back into the tiny sanctuary of trees in which she hid. Her fear was a palpable thing that scented the air and drove Griffon's hands to clench instinctively upon the hilt of his broad sword. He flashed the silver blade menacingly at those who dared arouse such fear in the Lady.

"Now, that would be close enough, I think." Griffon
warned, his gleaming sword pointed directly at the tall
thin man. His intuition told him this was their leader, the
more intelligent and therefore, the one to kill first. "I do
not seek to send you needlessly to your death."

"Your Lordship, noble warrior." It was, as predicted,
the tall, thin fellow who spoke. "We are poor, humble
men of the road, who must daily face the harsh inequities
life has presented us." His voice was soft and wheedling,
seeking to ingratiate, "Simply to find a crust of bread to
stave off starvation is like a gift from the Gods. Surely,
one so noble and generous as yourself would not begrudge
those as pitiful as ourselves some mere pittance." As he
spoke, they moved closer. "A scrap of bread, a rind of
cheese... a small morsel of female company." Little piggy
eyes, red rimmed and gleaming, sought to penetrate the
darkness behind Griffon, his meaning obvious.

"Very well, if it is death you seek so eagerly, I will
gladly oblige you." Griffon moved back, closer still to that
place where he had hidden Judith. His powerful arms
swung the huge broadsword effortlessly.

A cruel smile twisted Griffon's lips and quickly
became a frightening snarl. A cold finger of fear ran down
the spine of the one Griffon had identified as the leader.
His two companions were to stupid to be afraid. But he
was not stupid, no, on the contrary, he considered himself
quite clever. Sly enough to have survived the cruelty of
the road since he had taken to it at the age of seven. He
was now twenty and seven and living still. Not only did he
still live, but had all of his appendages intact. He ate
reasonably well—food could always be found for the

stealing. And occasionally, one could afford the purchase of a woman to warm the night. He intended to continue living into old age. He thought of the woman whose face he had seen peering out of the darkness and shook off the fear clutching at his gut. Perhaps, he was not as smart as he gave himself credit.

As if from a signal, all three attacked as one. Throwing stones as they advanced then swinging clubs, staying just out of range of Griffon's flashing sword. As Judith could testify, it would take more than a stone to bring Griffon down. His sword flashed as he faced the approaching men, keeping Judith's sanctuary ever at his back. A blow to the head forced Griffon back a step. The unlucky wielder of the club advanced, thinking himself at the advantage, only to find Griffon's blade there first. Even in death, he reached out for Judith, clutching at her cloak. No, perhaps he was not as cunning as he had given himself credit.

Griffon quickly severed the hand from his arm splashing her with the man's blood. Without their leader, the two remaining fell quickly with one blow, all but severing the head of one and glancing across the throat of the other. Nevertheless, wind was separated from body; both fell and lay still.

Griffon, too, was still as he surveyed the bloody scene; he had barely broken a sweat, although the adrenaline coursing through his body made his heart race. Without warning, he raised his bloodied sword and fist to the sky in a gesture of requital. He threw back his head and roared out his victory to the sky.

It was a wild, fearful sound, which froze Judith where she sat; her eyes round with shock, her mind numbed by the blood and carnage. She could only watch as Griffon performed what she knew instinctively to be an ordinance, a ritual with meaning known only to those men of war who perform it and to whatever God it is directed. Homage must be paid to the God who protects the warrior.

As Griffon helped Judith from her hiding place he took great care to keep himself between her and the bloody scene. He instructed her not to look, though she could not help but see the three lying dead or dying at her feet. Blood covered the ground. Griffon himself was again bleeding from the temple. Her hands flew to cover her eyes and her knees buckled. Griffon caught her up and carried her away. "Come, little one, down to the stream, splash cool water on your face. You will revive."

Leaving her at the stream, Griffon returned to the bloody scene. The cold water did help to revive her, although she could still picture that dying man reaching for her even as Griffon was wrenching his sword from the man's body. A shudder passed through her. Would she ever erase the memory of those three miserable wretches from her mind? If this was a dream, it was a terrifyingly realistic one.

"We must leave here." Griffon's manner was abrupt, he seemed angry. "A fresh storm approaches. The rain will come again soon and the light will leave us quickly. We must find shelter." Pulling her to her feet, Griffon pushed her at Lugh. After settling her on the horse in front of him, none-too-gently, he wheeled the horse round to the track, urging the massive animal into a fast trot. Judith averted her eyes as they passed the scene of carnage, not knowing Griffon had already removed the worst of it. They did not speak.

Judith leaned lightly against Griffon's chest. She could feel him stiffen against her shoulder; he did not welcome her as he had earlier. Did he blame her for the death of those men? Perhaps it was her fault. If she were not here, those men would not have attacked. It had been her they wanted. He had been forced to defend her. Alone, he could have mounted and ridden away or fought them off without killing them. God, *please, if this is a dream, let it end. What am I saying,* Judith thought to herself, *of course this is a dream and none of what just happened was real. Just a drug-induced dream!*

Five

Griffon was not angry, he was furious... with himself. He had wanted to kill those men. He had lusted for their blood, to defend the woman, Judith. Those three pitiful wretches had presented no danger to him; he could easily have driven them off, without the taking of life. Instead, he had reveled in their deaths, the letting of their blood by his sword, as any warrior would, to defend his Lady. But she was not his Lady. She belonged to another man. In truth, she had run from her husband, but she still belonged to the man. If she would but ask his protection, make her plight his. If she had but asked him to champion her... but she had not.

Griffon had felt her horror of the three which had approached them in the forest clearing. The thought of one of those diseased creatures so much as touching the hem of her gown had driven all thought from Griffin's mind, save the thought of killing. And that he had done, with skillful efficiency. The blood roared through his veins, he felt alive and very conscious of the woman seated before him. He realized Judith now leaned into him rather than shrinking from his touch. This, too, quickened his blood.

Could he now turn her over to her husband should they come upon him? He thought not.

He knew also, with little doubt, this was no sorceress. Not in his wildest imaginings could he see Judith wielding magical incantations and weaving spells. Which brought to mind another troublesome thought; what was he to do about the priest, Adolphus, when he returned to Dun Tirlough with Judith? There was no doubt Judith fit exactly the description the cleric gave. Adolphus would insist Judith was the witch he had seen in his vision. Perhaps if he were to appeal to Connault on Judith's behalf, his father might intercede. It was well known the old Lord had no liking for the Christian priest.

Griffon thought also of his wife Maeve, now dead these three years. He forced himself to steel his heart and his body against Judith. He tried to push all thoughts of her from his mind. They rode on in silence, climbing steadily through forested mountains. The silence between them was a living thing; one could almost touch it. There was not a single sign of civilization here except for the track they followed. The rains came again, a pounding sheet, obliterating all sight. Griffon gave Lugh his head, only the horse's instincts would keep them on the track. Judith huddled against him, wrapped in his mantle, his coarse, woolen cloak wrapped about them both. The rains, never lingering long, soon stopped and the weather cleared.

It was very nearly dark when they came upon an abandoned stone rath, a forester's cottage, only recently vacated, as the roof was still intact. Lowering Judith to the ground, Griffon led Lugh into a small paddock next to the cottage. Ignoring her presence, he turned his back to her.

His first thoughts must be the care of his mount. Lugh must be walked dry then brushed briskly with a coarse brush of boar's bristles, with close attention paid to his feet and the fine white feathering on each leg. Then he must be fed huge quantities of grass. A man's horse is his defense against a hostile world and must always be tended first.

His horse seen to, Griffon turned his attention back to Judith. He found her standing in the stream trying to wash the blood and dirt from her gown.

"Come away from there. The night draws quickly and you shall catch your death."

"I have to get this blood off of me, I can't stand it any longer. I stink of it."

"Very well. Get yourself inside. I'll fetch water for bathing and build a fire to warm you."

Judith's attempts to rinse her torn and bloody clothing had wet her through to the skin. Her teeth chattered between lips blue with cold. She reached up to let Griffon help her up the slippery banks of the stream. When he did not immediately take her hand, she looked up to find him staring at her, a strange look on his face. She was suddenly aware of the wet clinging negligee and, her cheeks flaming, tried to climb the steep, grassy slope unassisted, but could not manage the incline. As she began to slip back into the stream, Griffon caught her outstretched hand and pulled her up the slope. With one hand, he gripped her wrist, drawing her close. Judith stared up at him, aware of the great size of the man and the remoteness of the area.

With his other hand Griffon touched her face, hesitating when she flinched as he touched the bruises there, though he was as gentle as he knew how. The soft curve of her jaw, the swell of her breast, so like the satin feel of the wild orchids, which grew deep within the remotest parts of the forest. Her eyes seemed to draw him in, her gaze did not waiver, and it held him transfixed. The fragile fabric of her gown, thin as it was, separated beneath his fingers in an unconscious need to remove the offending barrier. The hard knot of her nipple rose against the palm of his hand. The soft, sweet touch of cool, white skin sent waves of heat through him.

A deep guttural moan escaped from deep within his throat. He lowered his head to hers, breaking the contact with her eyes, though it no longer mattered. He would carry the memory of emerald green eyes deep within his soul forever. His mouth sought hers, the rough leather of his tunic whispered against the soft skin of her breasts, her nipples pressed against his chest. He mistook her sharp intake of breath and the shudder which passed through her, for revulsion. Her body trembled beneath his hands. His grip relaxed, releasing her. His face was still inches from hers, her breath warm against his cheek.

"You have nothing to fear from me, my Lady." His lips brushed lightly against her neck, then again against the inside of her wrist "Now, go into the cottage, before I change my mind."

She gathered the tattered remains of her clothing and made for the stone rath. It had cost him much to release her. Never before had he hesitated to take a woman when he had the need, especially one who was as alone and unprotected as this one. But, he knew this was not a woman he could use and discard. Disgusted at his sudden surge of propriety, Griffon understood he had begun to have feelings for this woman. She was another man's woman and he was fast losing control of the situation. Shaking his head, he groaned as the motion awoke the wound on his left temple, which began to speak harshly to him. *By the Gods*, he thought, touching the spot where Judith had laid a rock against his head, *he did like a woman with fire*. Laughing aloud, his mood lightened as he set about bringing water and firewood into the cottage.

Night fell quickly in the forest and Griffon soon had a roaring fire built to push back the dark and warm the one room of the small rath. Griffon produced a clean linen shirt from his script and sat with his back turned so Judith might bathe. The sound of tearing cloth brought a faint shadow of a smile to his face. That would be the last he would see of that bit of silk. At a word from Judith, Griffon turned to find she had completed her bath. She had piled her dark satiny hair upon her head and secured it there using the heavy bronze brooch from his mantle. His shirt hung well below her knees and she had rolled the sleeves up to her elbows.

"Come sit here beside the fire, Griffon. Let me clean the wound on your head."

Griffon sat as docile as a kitten as Judith first tore the last of the gown into strips then used the strips to wash the blood from his face, daubing gently at first to loosen the dried blood, then more vigorously to clean the wound.

As she moved about him washing the blood from his face and chest, the light of the fire illuminated her form through the thin linen shirt. His desire for her returned, suddenly, with a physical force like a blow. Blood pounded in his ears. He pushed her roughly from him.

"Confound you, woman, it is more than a man can bear. Do you deliberately tempt me? If it is your intention to drive me to the edge of distraction, you have succeeded. Get yourself away from the fire, woman. Find a dark corner and settle lest you find yourself on your back. Doubtless, I could not stop myself so easily next time." He tossed her the fur rug from his bedroll to wrap herself in.

During the long night, Griffon rose often to tend the fire or to stand at the entrance to the small hut, restless at being confined in so small a space. She lay so near, he could hear her breathing. She did not sleep, he could tell by the way her breathing would stop whenever his pacing brought him near the place where she lay. Once he found himself standing over the woman. His thoughts returned again and again to the feel of her beneath his hands, imagining her body pressed against the full length of him.

His eyes, sought to find her slight form in the shadows. The firelight created shifting planes of darkness and light across her face. Her eyes, wide and staring, watched him continually. *Take her now*, he told himself *be done with it. This obsession is only lust, unsatisfied.* Griffin fought silently with himself, ever pacing the earth floor.

Finally, she slept, one small hand had escaped from the fur rug, palm up, and fingers curled slightly. Those fingers curled themselves around his heart. Come what may, he could not lose her, but he would not force her to come to him. This would be a long night indeed.

In the small hours before dawn, he found her again awake and watching him. She propped herself upon one elbow. "You must wonder what would cause me to run away from my husband as I did."

"The reason is plain, you wear the evidence upon your face and neck. There are many who believe a woman is nothing more than a man's property to do with as he chooses. My Grandmother's people believe differently. Women are considered to be the earthly embodiment of the Goddess herself, and so it used to be among the Celtic tribes as well. Women have led armies into battle, led their tribes to great victory. Andraste, the Great Queen of the North, it is said, was huge of frame and terrifying of aspect, with fiery red hair, which fell to her knees. She led the northern tribes into battle against the Eman Macha of Armagh. Many women still counsel their husbands in matters of war and state. I fear these things are changing."

"Still, I feel I have to explain. I'm usually not one to run away from trouble and I don't usually allow myself to be spirited away by strangers, but Peter frightened me so badly. I really thought he was going to kill me. I was so grateful when you said you had come to take me away from that place, I would have followed you anywhere. Anyway, I just felt you should know I am indebted to you for everything you have done for me. And I really hesitate to impose on you further, but I am just so frightened he will find me. Even here is this dream place. I know it sounds crazy, but what if he has followed me here?"

"Do you ask me to champion you, Lady? If it is so, then you need not fear. From this moment forth, you husband is my mortal enemy. He will not have you." At last, it was done; she had sought his protection. He willed the husband to appear before him now that he might slay the man, prove to Judith he was worthy of her trust in him, that he could protect her.

"Will you tell me about your home, Dun Tirlough?"

"There is little to tell. Dun Tirlough was built by the grandsire of my great grandsire, who was called Tirlough of the Red Beard. The bards tell of Tirlough as a fierce and mighty warrior. He slew many men in defense of his Lord and was rewarded with the land upon which Dun Tirlough now stands so he might build a fortress to defend the coast against those who would raid the coastal lands of his Lord. The fortress was built upon a solitary promontory of rock jutting out into the sea. The first dun was no more than a ring fort. A cashel of stone surrounded by a protective wall of earth and rock. Each generation has added more until it is as it appears today. It is the home of my people." But the Lady Judith slept; he doubted she had heard much of his tale. He sat back against the stone wall of the tiny hut and watched her sleep, thinking of his return to Dun Tirlough and the woman he brought with him. And he thought of the priest, Adolphus. Would he try to bring harm to Judith?

Six

The following morning, though Griffon had slept but a little, he awakened early to the smell of food cooking. Judith had rebuilt the fire and, in a small iron pot left by the cottage's former tenant, had prepared what she called an omelet. She had found a broody hen nesting near the cottage and filched her eggs then collected wild onions, and mushrooms, added the last bit of cheese from Griffon's script, and voila; omelet.

The smell of the cooking food had driven Griffon to circle about Judith like a wolf, until it was finally done to Judith's satisfaction, though he had not been prepared for how it would taste. This exotic egg and cheese concoction was new to his palate, however, it did not take long to finish his portion and go back to the pot for more.

"You have an appetite to match your size, larger than life."

"In truth, I must give credit to your skills in cooking, this was a meal unmatched in my recollection. Not only is the lady beautiful, but talented as well." It pleased him that she blushed and returned his smile with her own.

The meal over, Griffon led Judith to a narrow place in the stream, for she had insisted she must bathe before they resumed their journey. He found it strange she felt the need to bathe again so soon, but then he found many things about her strange. Until they had met the cutthroats in the wood yesterday, she had seemed unaware of the dangers which surrounded them. No lady would willingly venture into these woods without escort. She had seemed more frightened of her husband, one man, than the many perils of this remote wilderness. But then, he thought with a shrug, women in general he found to be uncommon strange creatures, alien to the male mind. He sat in silence, his back to her; watching the forest around them and pondering the wondrous creation that was woman and the many mysteries they represented.

Watching her dry her hair in the warmth of the sun, Griffon was overcome by contentment. He would stay in this very spot and hold time at bay, if such things were within his realm. He had never felt such peace. Even in his marriage to Maeve, there had been no peace.

Thinking of his wife, Griffon was torn by conflicting emotions. Taking a leather tunic from his script, he tossed it to Judith. Once she had pulled it over her head, over the linen shirt she wore, the tunic fell well below her knees, requiring her to belt it with a bit of leather from Lugh's livery.

"We must leave soon. The day grows old as we sit." Griffon allowed his raging thoughts to be known through his abrupt manner.

"Are you angry with me, Griffon? Is it that you believe the priest is right, that I'm a witch who has done some

injury to your father? I don't even know your father, why
would I want to harm him?"

Griffon was as confused as Judith about his feelings for
her. One moment his desire for her was a palpable thing,
the need to touch her a physical sensation akin to pain.
The next moment would bring Maeve to his thoughts and
he would become angry, but not angry with Judith, just
angry at his growing need for her. It was not her fault
Maeve's ghost stood solidly between them. It was not her
fault Griffon himself could not fathom his obsession with
a woman he had but met the day prior.

He touched a lock of her hair, and twisted it around his
finger, but only shook his head and lifted her up to Lugh's
broad back, then settled himself behind her. They traveled
through the morning in silence.

The forest began to thin noticeably and they had long
since begun their descent from the mountains. The narrow
forest track became a well-used, rutted path, which in turn
became a road. The heavy forest became a lush meadow
and evidence of civilization was everywhere.

They had stopped for the moment at the top of a gently
descending slope leading to a grassy bluff pasturing many
cattle. Stone fences lined each side of the track forming
paddocks.

Each paddock contained livestock, sheep, cattle or
horses. Some also held a tiny stone hut, and as they passed
these, the inhabitants swarmed out, shouting a greeting to
Griffon and his passenger. For the most part, they were
women and small children. The men and older children
being occupied in the fields and pastures called out to
Griffon from the fields they tended. All wondered about

the woman their young Lord brought with him, but none dared to ask.

The bluff ran along the top of a craggy cliff, the sea stretched beyond the horizon. Far in the distance, across the wild expanse of water, one could see the hazy blue line—the coast of Caledonia—Scotland. Judith recognized the scene immediately and looked about for the castle. It was not yet in sight.

A bend in the path led them around a finger of woods, which jutted out onto the bluff and there she stood, Dun Tirlough. The castle walls seemed to grow from the very cliff itself, like a living thing rooted in the rock upon which it stood.

As they neared the castle, the walls loomed far overhead, filling her vision. Armed men appeared along the top of the castle wall, shouting a warning.

"These are my Lord Father's men, there is no need to fear. I have fought and lived side by each since I was but ten and two."

Even as he spoke, a shout of recognition rose into the air. These same men filed out of the gatehouse and lined the barbican, which led to the tower gate. Each wanted to greet the well liked young Lord; each wanted to express their gratitude for Griffon's safe return from his journey. A few, those who knew Griffon well enough to presume upon his friendship, also congratulated him on the fine two-legged doe he had taken on this latest of hunting trips. Griffon's manner with these men was familiar and comfortable which spoke of a long association with this company of men.

"Griffon! Dun Tirlough is magnificent. Nothing could have prepared me for this."

The massive curtain wall, which protected the castle, rose ever higher as they entered the gate tower. A huge timber and stone wall towered into the air, pierced by five towers, the central the tower gate, where they were now entering, stood sentry over the castle entrance.

In her excitement, Judith momentarily forgot her conviction that this was nothing more than a dream brought on by delirium, and was fairly bouncing up and down where she sat. Her hand gripped Griffon's arm, and she pointed first to one building, then another, demanding to know what it was called, what was its purpose.

Griffon could only laugh, delighted and, infected by her excitement, he attempted to answer each question in turn.

"Those are called machicoulis, a parapet which protrudes from the top of the castle wall, where a man might stand and protect the wall from an enemy below. See, there is an opening to allow arrows to be loosed or stones dropped.

This structure is called the barbican; it is a fore-building which protects the tower gate. This is the inner bailey; my father's warriors live here and practice their battle skills there on the practice grounds."

Pulling her close, he pointed out each building explaining its use or function as they passed. It did not occur to Griffin to wonder why this woman was unfamiliar with the buildings and grounds of a castle enclosure. She was obviously of noble birth; neither her face nor body had been coarsened by work, her hands were delicate and soft.

Entering the inner barbican and crossing the palisade to the inner ward, Judith's mouth dropped open. The ruins of Dun Tirlough , which she had seen only two days earlier, gave no indication of the massive structure which was the Keep of Dun Tirlough. A huge rectangular stone structure with four towers, the far wall actually part of the protective curtain wall, gave out onto the cliff and the ocean below it. The two towers piercing the curtain wall were tremendous structures which soared well above the Keep itself. The two fore towers were smaller, though they too rose above the upper level of the Keep. The huge slabs of stone forming the steps leading up to the entrance to the Keep seemed to be carved from the very cliff itself. Griffon reined Lugh up suddenly. There, on the top step leading up to the Keep, Boann beside him, stood the old Lord, Connault, smiling broadly.

Seven

Castle Dun Tirlough

"Well, my Lord Father, it is good to see you have not allowed the death bed to slow yourself overmuch." Griffon clasped his father by the shoulders and kissed the old man on each cheek, then asked, on a more serious note, "You are well, father, you have recovered?"

"Aye, Griffon, you were no more than a day gone when I began to chaff at the constraints of the bed chamber, though your mother would keep me prisoner there yet another full day, before loosing the bonds." Boann chose not to notice her husband's wicked leer as he pressed her hand to his lips in a most uncourtly manner. He did appear most vigorous and healthy for a man so recently predicting his own demise.

Humoring her lecherous husband with an affectionate smile and a touch of her hand to his cheek, Boann regarded her son squarely. Not one to cower before her men, Boann was a woman of great strength and presence belied by her small stature. As a woman of royal Celtic blood, Boann's wit, and strength of character was a match

for any man. As a child of the old race, she had been
schooled in the ways of the priestess' of Danu, on the Isle
of Women. Her manner left little doubt in the minds of her
husband's retainers she expected to be obeyed and few
failed to jump at her command. There was very little
softness in Boann and that was reserved for her family. In
this instance, her affection for both husband and son was
readily evident in the softening of her features when she
addressed either.

"Griffon, you would present your guest?"

"Aye, Griffon." Connault threw an arm about his son's
broad shoulder. "Who is this you bring us, son? The priest
sent you to find the death crone and back you come with a
lovely prize."

"And what say I, but both be one, sire? I say young
Lord Griffon has found a prize, but the prize is the one for
which I sent him. There sits the sorceress which plagued
you, my Lord." Father Adolphus swept out of the
shadowed entrance to the castle Keep.

Until now, Judith had remained seated on Lugh's broad
back where Griffon left her, watching the encounter
between parents and son play out before her. Obviously
very close, there was much affection between them. The
words of the priest had shaken her out of her reverie. As
the priest came sailing down the castle steps, robes
billowing around him, eyes squinting in the bright sun,
and coming to what he obviously felt to be a dramatic
flourish at the bottom of the steps, pointing up at Judith as
he denounced her. Before she could recover her wits to
defend herself, Griffon had descended the steps, bearing
down upon the frail old cleric, a fierce scowl spreading

across his face. To his credit, old Adolphus did not so much as flinch but held his ground.

"You are mistaken, priest, moreover, a fool who quakes at stories to frighten children." Griffon helped Judith down from the horse's back then, placing himself between her and the priest, turned back to confront the old crow. "I found naught at the place which you sent me and would have counted the journey a loss were it not that I did come upon this Lady, abandoned by the roadside, in danger of being set upon by thieves or worse. Nay, priest, there was no witch at the place to which I was sent. I did bring this Lady here to this house for refuge, not to suffer beneath your evil tongue, old man." It plagued Griffin very little that he had chosen this small lie to forestall the priest's accusations.

"It is a trick. A ruse to confuse you and enlist your aid." The old man fairly squeaked with indignation. He had counted upon the discovery of a witch, which he, Adolphus, could manipulate to his own advantage. He had hoped his dealing with a demonic force would elevate his standing with the elder Lord and his headstrong young son and perhaps lead them both to the Christian doctrine. Yet this Lordling had foiled his plan, and this was not a wise thing to do.

"I tell you she is a sorceress, a demon who will wreak havoc upon this noble clan. Her presence is not to be tolerated in this Christian household." Too late, Adolphus realized he had overstepped himself.

"Silence priest, you forget yourself." Connault's voice boomed out at them from the top of the steps out and across the inner ward. The hounds in the kennels whined and cowered, the horses in the stable shied, murmuring softly to each other for comfort, restless at the anger in their master's voice.

"I am Lord of this place and all you see, for as far as you see and beyond. I will say who may be sheltered under my roof. You are here by the good wishes of my eldest living son and heir, who believes himself a Christian. So be it, but do not overstep yourself priest." Lord Connault had spoken.

Father Adolphus, purple with rage at how his manipulations had turned on him as a rabid dog that would bite his own master's hand, managed to inclined his head in obeisance, gathered his anger around him with his skirts and withdrew once again into the shadows.

"Griffon, bring your guest forward where we might better see her."

"Aye, my Lord, with pleasure." With great ceremony, Judith was presented to the Lady Boann and Lord Connault. She was surprised at the formality of the introduction and remembered to curtsey as Peter had instructed her.

As an enlightened woman of the twentieth century, Judith was totally unprepared for what happened next. Connault inquired of his son what he intended to do with her.

"I lay claim to her as is my right, my Lord. She is abandoned by her husband and has no clansmen to protect and shelter her." Judith's cheeks flamed with embarrassment. "I have bloodied my sword with the slaying of three men in protection of her life and honor. Lady Judith has sought my protection, which I have given freely. The woman is mine and I will face any man who would challenge my claim."

"And what of this husband should he seek the return of his woman?

"I do not fear to meet the man in fair combat, my Lord. I would as soon have her a widow and free of any obligation."

"So be it, it will be done upon the Druids' return." With that said, the two men descended the steps and made for the practice fields, leaving Judith standing on the castle steps.

Father Adolphus, having watched the proceedings from shadow, scuttled off on a mission of his own.

So be it! So be it! How dare they! She turned to Boann for support. The last two days had been entirely too much. Weary, sick with fear, confused and alone, tears stung her eyes but did not fall. She was stunned by what appeared to be a sudden transformation which seemed to take over Boann. She found herself alone with the dark Boann, A greatly magnified Boann. Though they were much the same stature, she found herself immensely in awe of the woman, for no apparent reason, except she seemed... larger. No, that's not right. She appeared to emanate power—she almost shimmered, like the heat waves coming up from the pavement on a 100-plus degree day. Griffon's mother seemed to change, somehow grow, before her very eyes. It must be a trick, a crazy, inexplicable, fascinating trick. Just as suddenly, Judith was sure Boann used some... something... an illusion was somehow created to make her appear intimidating, somehow larger than herself.

"I don't intend to be rude, but, well..." tentative, but charmed by the idea of magic, her threatened tears forgotten, Judith gathered her courage, "... how do you do that? Make yourself look bigger like that?"

Judith's candor startled Boann into delighted laughter; her dark eyes reflected her amusement, as her illusion melted around her. The glamour had never failed to bring a reaction from any who had been witness to Boann's magic. Usually fear, sometimes something a little darker... like envy, but never, outside of the initiated, never curiosity.

"It is a small glamour, a simple illusion, taught to me by my mother. Not many see through the magic, simple as it is." She liked this girl; there was strength in her. There would be time enough to see just how much.

Calling to her women, Boann soon had Judith deposited in a steaming tub of hot soapy water. Her son's mantle and clothing folded over her arm, Boann wondered at Judith's lack of the proper woman's attire and her need to wear borrowed apparel. It was, perhaps, best not to ask. Not one to remain in the dark for long, she was, however, intelligent enough to know when to ask certain questions and when to leave things as they stood... at least for now.

~ * ~

Griffon and his father had crossed the Keep's inner ward, passed through the inner barbican, and entered the outer bailey. They stood now at the practice grounds where Griffon's comrades were paired off and locked in what appeared to be heated battle, and what in reality was more horseplay than serious practice.

"What is it, Griffon, you are troubled?" Connault, though often seeming oblivious to the machinations of others, saw much more than he was given credit.

"Make no mistake, Father, this time I will take no chances. This woman will be given no chance to prove faithless, as Maeve did. I will not allow it. I am but two days in her presence and already my life is neatly held within the palm of her hand. She has but to close her fist upon it to destroy me utterly. Three years it has taken to recover from the infidelity of my wife and I did not hold her near or so dear as this one. This will remain between you and I, Father, I'll not have this woman know she controls me so."

"Griffon, you do not know Maeve was unfaithful to you. You yourself told me you knew nothing of these rumors until after her death in childbirth. Do not visit unfounded blame on this other. Son, I saw you laugh today for the first time in three years, as you entered the inner ward. And your Lady, she can scarce keep her eyes from you. This is a love match; it is not like what you had with Maeve. Accept it and be grateful for it. Now get yourself on to the field where your comrades will see to it you have little time to think of women. Go now; work off these misgivings on the practice field. See there, they await you."

Connault watched with affection, as his youngest son was welcomed among his fellows with great shouts and horseplay. His thoughts, very much like those of Boann, were on the woman his son had brought to their home.

A striking pair those two had made as they had entered the inner ward of Dun Tirlough. Two shining dark heads,

Griffon's bent low nearly touching Judith's, as he whispered into her ear, pointing out the buildings of the inner ward. Griffon's crimson cloak, which Judith wore wrapped about her, reflected its color upon her pale cheek. Or perhaps it was what Griffon whispered into her ear that had awakened the blush there.

Connault and Boann had watched, amazed, as their once deeply unhappy son had approached the castle steps. Both had seen immediately the transformation in their son. He laughed, his eyes flashed. Gone was the dark, deathly silence in his eyes—at last, he seemed happy. Small wonder they had eagerly accepted this stranger into their home.

Connault thought, not for the first time, it would be good for Griffon to take a wife again. Connault had thought his son would take another wife soon after Maeve's death, but it had not happened. Instead, Griffon had believed the stories of the infidelity of his now dead wife, and he chose to believe all women adulterous by nature and unable or unwilling to be faithful. But this day, Connault had heard his son's laughter as he had ridden up to the steps of the Keep, speaking in animated fashion to the woman who sat before him, wrapped in his cloak. This woman had made their son smile, it was enough, and they would welcome her with arms stretched wide. Connault laughed aloud, causing heads to turn in his direction. Indulgent smiles met the old Lord's laughter. The old man was known to enjoy his own thoughts very much.

Father Adolphus, too, had sought out the company of others, the only other avowed Christians in the family household, though there were a few among the men at arms and their families. Connault's oldest living son and heir, Bryon, had been fostered in a Christian household and, until the death of Connault's two first-born sons in battle, had been intended for the church. Bryon's wife, Annu, had also been raised a Christian. Being the eldest daughter of Bryon's foster father, they had been betrothed and quickly married when word had reached them of the death of Bryon's elder brothers. As his father's heir, he was expected to give up his thoughts of entering the church, marry and produce an heir of his own.

It was natural Adolphus sought them out now, lamenting the misfortunes which would befall the household.

"That unholy wench is not to be tolerated in a Christian household. God will call down his vengeance upon any and all who would shelter her."

"Did He not say vengeance should be left to Himself, Adolphus?"

An innocent enough query, however, it was not what Adolphus wanted to hear from his patron. Bryon was, as usual, immersed in his study of the latest religious tract he had managed to acquire. His answers had been, at best, perfunctory, barely managing to meet the requirements of courtesy, and entirely unsatisfactory for Father Adolphus, who was desperate for some validation of his place within the household. He was not an evil man, but desperation and ignorance can often make one appear so. This last comment from Bryon was too much and so he turned to the other Christian in Connault's household; Bryon's young and very pregnant wife, Annu.

"I tell you, I have seen the evil these unclean ones have wrought. They prey upon the weak, the old. Once this one has established her hold on this house, the innocent will suffer."

Adolphus was soon concentrating all his attention upon Annu who gave the old cleric her complete and undivided attention. Not wanting to disappoint his audience, Adolphus regaled young Annu with tales of deviltry and demonic mischief, all the while thinking what a pious and devoted Christian the child was. Adolphus had come from the household of Bryon's foster parents and Annu's education, such as it was, had been his responsibility. She was, therefore, well acquainted with his stories of pagan worship and the evils of men.

~ * ~

Boann and Triona had by now comforted and reassured Judith who was being vigorously toweled dry. Triona, though younger than Judith by several years, was greatly excited by the arrival of another young woman in the Keep. Judith also sensed a friend in Griffon's young sister.

"I do hope we might become friends, Lady Judith. Annu is no fun a t'all. She spends ever so much time on her knees in the chapel. When not at devotions, she is sewing, embroidering, and weaving. No fun a t'all, a t'all."

Triona had picked up a comb and began running it through Judith's long black hair.

Boann chided her young daughter affectionately, "I am not surprised at your lack of enthusiasm for household duties, wild one. A six-year-old child makes straighter stitches, Triona. Ach, I blame myself. You were my youngest and I did indulge you overmuch. You were always more interested in following your brothers about than is proper for a young lady. Now, child, tell me how you came to be found by my son in such a state."

Boann took over the braiding of Judith's hair from Triona as Judith began to tell them of her meeting with Griffon at the sacred well and the events, which had brought her there.

"And so, you asked the Gods to help you, child. But why do you follow the old ways?" Boann had immediately picked up upon the small lie Griffon had spoken of his finding Judith. Her son's feelings for this girl were deep enough for him to lie; something Griffon rarely, if ever, did.

"In the end, aren't all Gods the same? We call them by different names, give them different purposes and direction, but when it comes right down to it, they are all one and the same."

Boann nodded her understanding. "What was it you asked of the Goddess, child?"

"Acceptance, I guess. For a man who would love me, respect me, a man who wouldn't question my need to explore and understand the world. I don't want to be a piece of art that some man has collected to ornament his home. Do I ask too much?"

"In this world we inhabit, child, anything a woman asks for is too much, if the man who owns her deems it so. So, you do not ask, you take. If you want respect, take it, do not ask for it. You show by your actions what you are willing to tolerate. You have strength in you child. I have seen it. The Goddess, Danu, has seen it. Which is why she has brought you here. Your fate and Griffon's are tied one to the other and Danu has a purpose for you both.

"Enough talk of fate and the Goddess; what is to be will be. Let us get you dressed; it is time for the evening meal. Triona, Judith shall share your bed and chamber. Off you go, dinner will be prepared soon." Boann hustled the two girls out of the bathing chamber.

"Judith shall have your good blue gown, Triona. You outgrew it before it had been worn but twice. It should fit Judith well."

Eight

Judith and Triona ran up the mural stairs, laughing, arm in arm, already fast friends. The Maiden's Tower could only be reached by way of the mural stair within the thickness of the wall. The stair led from the first level, which was actually the second story of the Keep. The first story, being given over to storage and cellarage, was also reached by way of the mural stair, then up to the next level leading to the bathing chamber, which they had just left, then up to Boann and Connault's chamber. They had to pass through the Lord's Chamber to enter the Maiden's Tower stairway which led down two levels and up one level to Triona's and Judith's room and from there to the tower roof.

From the roof, one could see for miles in any direction. Being one of the two tallest towers, you could even see over the inner ward wall and into part of the outer bailey. One could also see far out to sea where the coastline of Caledonia was no more than a blue smudge on the horizon.

Once in the chamber she was to share with Triona, Judith was able to look around at her surroundings. The floor had a thick covering of reeds, the walls were covered in bright tapestries; one depicting a bloody battle, the other covered over with intricately intertwined knots. A small brazier burned coal to take the chill from the room. Judith could not help but notice a magnificent bed piled high with the softest of fur rugs. She wrapped herself in a particularly cozy one and lay down on the plush down mattress to listen as Triona chattered on. How had Judith and Griffon met? What country did Judith hail from? Were Judith and Griffon lovers? This last brought a blush to her cheeks—and a definite, if somewhat hasty, response of, *no!* At last, Triona's chatter fell into a soft and pleasant murmur.

Absolute comfort combined with the trials of the last two days, and soon Judith was fast asleep. She slept through the rest of the day and that night. She had some vague recollection of Triona snuggling down next to her beneath the furs.

She opened her eyes once to find a pair of the blackest eyes she had ever seen peering at her closely. Although the apparition belonging to those eyes was apparently standing, they met her own almost on a level. At first, Judith thought one of the castle's children had wandered in, there being many children running about the Keep. Did the child need help? But when Judith made to rise and inquire what the matter could be, a tiny withered hand made up of brittle twig bones and parchment brown skin signed for her to remain as she was. When the tiny woman spoke, it was the voice of a sweet wind whispering through the trees.

"Do not alarm y'self, nor this house. I needs must see thee m'self before thy journey continues."

The old woman stepped slightly forward so the dying light from the brazier lit her face. A truly ancient, little, nut-brown face near hidden beneath a dark blue cowl regarded her solemnly. Judith wished she could see her visitor more clearly. As if on command, the cowl slid to the old woman's shoulders, revealing long gray wisps of hair. Tiny bits of twig, dried leaves and flowers clung to her hair and clothing. Judith's first impression was of one who had traveled through dense, grasping forest to reach here, but on closer inspection, She saw the flowers, leaves, and twigs were carefully arranged. Not the unkempt, forgetfulness of old age about personal cleanliness, more like an adornment. Almost as if she were a tiny little bit of the forest which, having been given life, chose to ornament herself with that forest which had given her life. Her face, deeply grooved by age, very much resembled the living bark of an ancient conifer tree. The old woman smiled, as if she had heard Judith's thoughts aloud, a beatific, stunning smile. Toothless as it was, it lit her face, transforming her little wrinkled form into that of a... Goddess?

"Are you she?" Tentative, afraid to startle the apparition and afraid for herself, Judith whispered, "Are you the Goddess, Danu?"

"Non, child. I be thy guide to where thee need go. Come thee here or go thee there, I be wi' thee ever'where. She sent thee to me, but it falls to me to judge thy worth."

"I don't understand." But she thought she did understand. A vagrant, from out of the woods nearby. Senile, perhaps, she had made her way into the castle. Maybe one of the serving women had taken pity upon the old woman and let her into the castle for food and shelter and she had wandered up here.

"Thee marry wi' the boy for now. 'Tis enough to start. Get thee to me, when thee can. We begin then."

She passed her hand over the brazier and the flame flared briefly, illuminating the old woman's face. No, not senile. There was intelligence in those eyes, a deep knowing, and what else? A calculating gleam, perhaps? The light faded and the room darkened. Try as she might, Judith could not see the old woman, nor did she sense movement.

"Who are you?" she whispered, frightened in spite of herself, unaccountably frightened. There was no response. "What is your name? How do I find you?"

"When the time come, follow thy thoughts to where they lead thee." Where had the voice come from? Behind her, no, couldn't have. There, beside the bed? No. Inside her head? Just a whisper, like someone had leaned close to her ear to speak quietly to only her, but closer. What was it the old woman was trying to tell her? Where had she come from and how had she gotten this far into the Keep without being stopped? More important, where had she gone and how had she disappeared as though before Judith's very eyes?

She awakened to daylight streaming through the narrow loops, which passed for windows in the thick stone wall. What time was it, how long had she slept? Judith recalled her visitor during the night. A dream, that's all. It had already begun to fade, and she was ravenous.

Nine

"My Lord, Connault," Etaine ni Ruath, Druid priestess and daughter of Mog Ruath, Connault's Druid adviser, entered the Great Hall chamber. She crossed to the vast fireplace where Connault and his sons held council with Mog Ruath. Her entrance was regal. Caught back in a jeweled clip, dark auburn hair, like burnished copper, fell down her back in a flawless sheet, well past her narrow waist. Her gown was the dark indigo of the priestess, though made of the finest of wool. It fit her like a second skin, accentuating voluptuous curves. Over her gown, she wore an overcoat of spun silk, dyed to match the indigo of her gown. The cuffs and neckline were embroidered with mystic symbols and incantations. All eyes turned to watch Etaine approach. Even her father, Mog Ruath, whose thin chest swelled with pride at the effect his child's entrance had made, her every move effortless, elegant.

The Druidess made a small obeisance to Connault, the gesture somehow conveying the impression of a great gift bestowed rather than an act of respect. Icy blue eyes sought and found Griffon, the others in the room forgotten.

"So, Griffon." Slender fingered hands encircled Griffon's arm, a caressing gesture. "The outer bailey, indeed the entire countryside speaks of nothing but this clanless waif you have championed. Where is the child, surely you have not taken her into the castle Keep. We shall all be murdered in our beds. Who knows how the child was raised."

"I fear rumors do not always convey truth, Etaine; small as a child she may be, the Lady Judith is no child, of that I assure you. The Lady was abandoned by the road, at the mercy of thieves and cutthroats. I found her in need of my protection which I gave to her gladly." Patting her hand indulgently, they moved into the dining chamber with the others.

"And what of the Lady now, Griffon?" Hugging his arm to her breast, Etaine moved against Griffon. Nearly as tall as he, her eyes met his on the same level.

"We did discuss that very thing just now." Etaine's sharp eyes took in the empty spot Griffon kept at his right side even as he seated Etaine at the table.

The seating at meals was strictly ordered, one's place within the clan was reflected in where one was placed at the table.

The head table was placed upon an elevated dais nearest the fire. Connault, with Boann at his right hand, sat at the center, their place being closest to that same fire. Mog Ruath, as his adviser, sat at Connault's left. Then, Bryon and his Lady, with Father Adolphus at the end. On

Boann's right, until now, had sat Griffon with Etaine seated at his right; honored guests would be seated next. It had been implied by this arrangement that when Griffon was ready to wed again, Etaine would be his choice, though no formal arrangement had been made. By moving Etaine further down the table, keeping the place directly to his right free, the implication was clear. A stinging blow to Etaine's place within the clan.

"My Lord Father will make the announcement this night."

"What! You cannot mean you intend to be wedded to this woman. What do you know of her?" Hard, pale blue eyes flashed danger for but a second. "Take the wench as a mistress, bed her if you must, but to give your name to some unknown slut..." Realizing she tread unsteady ground, Etaine cut short her diatribe. Too late.

"You go too far, Etaine. We have been children together. You are my friend and like a sister to me, but I'll no' tolerate insult to my Lady."

Taking Griffon's arm again, Etaine's tone became honeyed, conciliatory. "It is just that I have seen you hurt before, Griffon. It is true, you are like my own brother, indeed, if your brother Ciran had not been killed, then brother and sister we would be. I wish only to protect you from another like Maeve."

"I am no fool, Etaine. I have no wish to return my hand to the fire."

"Where is the Lady? Does she join us?" Even as she spoke, Judith and Triona entered the Great Hall.

Judith looked pale and uncertain. Triona had brushed her hair until it shone, the tiniest of braids along each temple, pulled together at the back of her head, held the shining wave which was covered by a long silk veil held down by a thin circlet of gold about her forehead. Her pale skin was made even paler still by the deep emerald green of the borrowed gown. It was of the finest linen, covered by a kirtle of the softest doeskin, caught about her middle by a silk girdle and fastened with a beaten gold clasp just below her navel. Soft leather shoes stitched over with tiny seed pearls covered her feet. Every head in the room turned to see the woman everyone had heard of but few had seen. Judith hesitated, unsure of her place at this assemblage and uncomfortable with the sudden silence her entrance had caused, then found Griffon already there at her side, as he had always seemed to be, his hand at her elbow to guide her to her place at his side.

"Why do they stare at me? Have I done something wrong?" Whispering softly to Griffon so others might not be aware of her discomfort, Judith accompanied Griffon to their place at the head table.

"It is nothing more than envy. The women stare because they are but coarse cloth compared to my Lady. The men stare, because it is their ladies, which are cut from that coarse cloth. You tremble, are you ill? Perhaps it is too soon after the distress of the last few days. This is too much for you?"

"No, no. I'm fine. Just a little warm." Boy, was that an understatement. Judith had admitted to herself that while they had been traveling, she had felt a definite attraction for Griffon. After all, what red-blooded woman wouldn't? He was a dark, good looking and powerful man, but there had been something else. A magnetism. However, she had fully expected that after a good night's rest her old practical self would take over and that would be the end of any foolish notions she might feel for Griffon. Likewise, she had expected his desire for her to be diverted elsewhere once they had arrived. After thinking about it, she had expected him to reconsider the marriage. But now, seeing him again, having him touch her, even though it was just a touch on the arm, or a brief brush against the small of her back with his hand, having him speak sweet words into her ear, she felt the heat rising in her.

Connault rose, bellowing for silence, as the entire gathering had erupted into animated discussion and he would have what he was to say heard by all assembled. When silence was restored, Connault spoke.

"According to the laws of the Brehon, as they have been interpreted to me, a Lady who finds herself without male kin or clansman to keep and protect her and see to her proper disposition, becomes the responsibility of the Lord of the land. It is also said that if this Lady be championed by a warrior who would use his sword to protect her, that warrior, by right, may lay claim to her through the offer of marriage."

The Great Hall echoed with voices raised, they now knew what was coming. Drinking cups banged upon the massive tables to show their approval. Many believed Griffon had waited too long to wed again. Etaine's face revealed little of the rage, which churned within her.

Outwardly calm, even managing to smile convincingly, her countenance belied the inner storm. Banging his ale mug upon the table, sending its contents spraying across the table and onto those sitting at the table directly below, Connault again silenced his gathered clansmen.

"Therefore, as is required by law, I make this announcement before all who gather here. My youngest son, Griffon mac Connault, by right of law will claim the Lady Judith as his wife. Custom dictates that a fortnight will be set aside for any challenge to this claim. If at the end of those fourteen days there is no challenge, they shall be joined. It is done."

The hall erupted into chaos and much toasting ensued. Griffon leaned close to Judith's ear so only she could hear.

"What say you, Judith? Would you have me as your husband? It is true I am not my father's heir, but I am not without resources. I have my own land and manor. While my coffers do not rival my father's, my fortune has been made and I may offer you a life not without its comforts. I would have you willing and not come to me against your will. In truth I would as soon be greeted each night by a kiss as by a rock across my temple."

Deeply touched by Griffon's asking for her approval, Judith was well aware women in the Dark Ages had very little to say regarding their fate, it was not necessary for the bride to be a willing one. And yet he had asked her if she wanted him. Looking up into deep gray eyes, she saw something there, a silent plea, there for but the briefest of moments, then gone.

"I care very little for fortunes and property. But tell me, what was it your father, Lord Connault, meant by a challenge?"

Watching her closely, Griffon's eyes narrowed slightly and the barest flames of anger flared for a moment. Why did she ask about the challenge? Did she have a lover somewhere that she hoped might come for her? He had allowed this woman to see a small corner of his need for her, was it a mistake? Breathing deeply to calm the small flicker of dark thoughts, Griffon responded.

"Any man who feels he has a claim may challenge me for you. It is the law; your kinsman does not give you to me, therefore, any who wishes may challenge. Why do you ask? Is there one you would prefer?"

"The thought that someone, some stranger, might walk in here and demand I be given to him frightens me. I don't want anyone else, only you."

His face darkened, did she mock him? Could this be the truth she speaks? How does one ever judge the truth in a woman's words? The flood of emotions held so long in their dark, icy prison, those two small words released would not be held back any longer. They threatened to choke him if he did not release them. Two simple words... only you. He sought desperately to bring forward images of the unfaithful Maeve, tried to call to mind the stories of her infidelity. It did not work. His thoughts were in turmoil. Was he to be so easily brought to heel by the words of one small woman? *By the Gods, I have lost all control of my life. My soul is given over to the whims and desires of a woman.* Bringing Judith's hand close, he pressed it tightly against his forehead, forcing himself, by shear strength of will, to speak the thing which he needed most to know.

"I take that to mean you will have me, Lady?"

"Until death and beyond." Until she spoke, Judith had not realized how deeply she had fallen in love with Griffon, that she meant every word she said. Could one fall in love with a dream? So, what did it matter this was not reality; that she probably lay bleeding and near death at the bottom of the Druid well. If that were to be her fate, then what harm did it do to spend her remaining time here in this dream place she had created for herself? She did not dwell on the thought for long, as it was a fleeting one.

Griffon pressed his lips against the soft flesh of her palm. She was surprised and taken aback by the naked desire in his eyes and felt her own blood responding to him in kind. If not for sharing Triona's chamber, Judith felt with certainty she would have a passionate visitor this night. She would not have turned him away.

Neither noticed Etaine. Though her face was as pale as linen, she appeared to be calm. A single drop of blood formed between the fingers of a clenched fist, falling to the table. Her thoughts, indeed her entire consciousness was riveted upon the pale, slight form, which quite literally sat between her and what she most desired.

Most everyone at the gathering had studiously ignored the two lovers, and it was obvious to all present that this was a love match.

The clearing of a throat at Judith's shoulder brought both of them back to their present surroundings; the food had arrived. The amount and variety of food and beverage served at the meal astounded Judith. Fish and fowl, roasts of beef and pork, a variety of vegetables, breads, cheeses and fruit, as well as ale and wine. She and her soon-to-be husband shared a trencher between them. Picking the choicest bits for Griffon from each serving platter as the servants carried them around the table, Judith, however, ate little. She was fascinated by the activity around her. While they ate, hounds and small children wove their way under and around the tables. The children followed the dogs, the dogs watched closely for a delicacy to be offered or dropped. Musicians sat in a corner and played softly—a low, lilting melody. Largely unnoticed by all. Occasionally the roughhouse between young men would go beyond play and erupt into something more serious. Lord Connault would shout a warning at the miscreants or throw something at one or the other if they did not heed.

Even so, the meal seemed to go on and on. Embarrassingly close to falling asleep over her trencher, Judith was grateful for the arrival of what seemed to be the evening's entertainment. An elderly gentleman in baggy breeches and a tunic twice his size, settled himself in the center of the room and began to recount the history and glory of the Ulaid in the form of a poem. The intricate beauty of form the poem took entranced her. She learned from Griffon the old man was called Dhonaill, a vate or historian, who traveled the country and kept an oral history of the people. The old man was well respected, as were all those of his profession, and was welcomed into any household.

When he reached the history of this house, his poetic praise was extravagant, glorifying the house of Connault, his ancestors, and his sons. It was here Judith learned of the death of Connault's two eldest sons, Ciran and Lomnae, in the battle of Cuailnge, how Bryon came to be his father's heir and the great warrior Griffon had proven to be, even at his young age. She was delighted to hear her own story recounted as Griffon bravely fought off an army of cutthroats and thieves to save the honor of the Lady Judith whose beauty was told of in legendary terms, but blushed and hid her face when he told of her arrival at Dun Tirlough, clothed only in the male garb they had used to disguise her in order to secret her through the territory of the hated Eman Macha. The poem ended with Connault's announcement of Griffon's marriage claim and the period of waiting which would ensue. What the story lacked in accuracy, it more than made up for in action and adventure, as well as the elegance and beauty of its presentation. The meal complete, the entertainment over, Judith pled fatigue so she might be allowed to leave gracefully.

Griffon accompanied his sister and Judith to the Maiden Tower stair but no further. As Judith discovered, no man, save the Lord of the house, was allowed beyond the base of the stairs. She was, perhaps, more than just a little disappointed she would not be receiving any feverish midnight visits. Griffon seemed suddenly awkward, almost shy. Hardly the passionate and fervid man she had come to know. She wondered what could have changed his mood so quickly and wanted to see that passion again. She caught his hand in hers as he turned to leave her.

"Where I come from, when a man and woman are to be married, it is customary for the engagement to be sealed with a kiss."

"You tempt me beyond reason, woman. Get yourself to your chamber. And you as well, little sister."

Griffon swatted at a laughing Triona, who easily dodged her brother's playful attempt to catch her. Watching his sister ascend the tower stair until she disappeared round the curve of the tower, Griffon turned back to Judith.

"Do you still stand here? Your bed is there, at the top of these stairs." His scowl was in truth only half-hearted and did nothing to dissuade her.

"I am serious, Griffon, you must kiss me."

Running her hands over his arms and shoulders, she could feel his muscles tense beneath her touch. So great was his height above her own, she could not put her arms around his neck when he held himself erect. Grabbing a handful of tunic in each hand, she tugged playfully.

Unprepared for the swiftness of his movements, the force of him drove the breath momentarily from her body as he lifted her from her feet. His mouth firm against hers, he pressed her hard against the wall. She did not fight. Judith clung to him matching the force of his passion. She felt him relax in her arms, his mouth no longer bruising, but now devouring. His hands against her back held her against him. His lips explored her silken neck and wondrous hollow at the base of her throat. He spoke his passion aloud, though Judith heard it only as a sweet murmur. He bit gently at her hard nipples which pushed against the thin woolen gown. Breathing hard, Judith wrapped her arms around his neck, speaking to him of her need for him, dangerously close to abandoning any modestly she might possess. She would have him take her right here, right now.

But it was Griffon who pulled back, gently setting her back upon unsteady feet. Barely touching her, he brushed his fingers over the swell of her cheek. His voice was thick and lust still clouded his eyes.

"Go now, before I dishonor myself and my family and bed you right here on this stone floor."

He whirled on his heel and left her, braced by the wall, her lips swelling slightly where he had crushed them against his, watching his retreating back. He did not turn to look at her as he walked away.

Ten

Early the next morning Judith rose with the sun, eager to explore her new surroundings. She woke her young friend and companion. The girls had whispered well into the night but Judith was too excited to sleep past sunrise. She had been promised a tour of the castle and the surrounding forest. Triona proved as eager to show off her home as Judith was to see it. They dressed carefully, Judith because she was eager to please Griffon, Triona because she was young and pretty and wanted all the young men to know it. The girls had thought to leave the castle grounds early and explore the countryside at their leisure. They had not anticipated Griffon's obsession with his young bride-to-be.

At the foot of the mural stair, they found a guard awaiting them. Griffon had assigned the man to accompany them whenever they might leave the castle Keep, for their protection, it not being safe for young ladies of their position to travel beyond even the inner ward, the man informed them. Judith did not much care for the idea, but considering her experience in the forest, assumed it was necessary. Triona merely shrugged and, taking Judith's hand, led the way to the kitchen, where they would pack bread, cheese, and a small container of ale for three.

If Judith had expected the castle to be silent at such an early hour, she was mistaken. The kitchen at least, was a hive of activity. It would seem the labor of the kitchen never really stopped altogether. Someone was always working, preparing, stocking, loading, unloading, or accounting for something. The room itself was a large rectangle. In the center of the room stood an immense oak table for the preparation of meals. At present, Baker was involved, up to her elbows, in the day's bread. Behind her, through a narrow archway, within a small niche, a scullery boy was stoking the fires for the bread ovens, making them ready for the dozens of loaves of bread, which would be consumed by the household that day.

To the left of the table was the fire pit. An immense stone pit, large enough to roast a full-sized spitted steer and a pig side by side—at the same time! As well as the odd pots of stew simmering, soups bubbling, porridge cooking, which another cook was basting, stirring, and turning, for the day's meals. Huge stacks of wood were piled high against a far wall, waiting to be fed to the blazing coals. Beyond the fire pit, through another narrow arch, stood several vast barrels, the tops of which stood higher than a man could reach; of wine and beer, no doubt. There beside them stood a now idle press, used in the making of the wine, she supposed.

To the right of the table stood one of the single most important items in the room; the well. What it must have taken to dig down through an untold number of feet of rock to find a water source was overwhelming. Yet there it was, with a scullery maid cranking away at the handle to bring up bucket after bucket of fresh water to keep the immense household going. High overhead wooden platforms lined the walls, which were stacked high with sacks of storage grain, apples, oranges, potatoes, onions and every other conceivable form of storage fruit or vegetable. Up a small flight of steps, was a storage room of more precious fair. Wheels of cheese, exotic spices, and sugar. Those items which cost dearly and were rationed closely by the lady of the house. Scattered around and under the table were more sacks of produce waiting to be prepared. Judith felt overwhelmed, and perhaps, more than a little useless. She was unused to being in the midst of such intense activity and not being a part of it.

"Triona, what am I to do while I am here?"

"I know not what you mean, Judith." She could see her friend was puzzled by her question, because Judith recognized the troubled look in her eyes.

"Everyone here seems to have a job, a function. Your mother has women who make the cloth, sew the clothing, and make fancy embroidery and tapestries, women who cook, and care for the children. Men who make furniture, mend equipment, make weapons, and raise the food you eat. Everyone does something useful. I can do none of these things. I am useless in this household."

"Judith, you are to be my brother's wife. You will bear his children, run his house, and manage his property when he is at war, even as my mother does manage my father's lands. Granted, my brother's holding are not so vast as father's, but they will do, and there will be little time to wonder what you shall do, I warrant."

"But I wish to be more than just the keeper of a man's home and children, although I agree, under these conditions, that is a full time job in itself. However—"

She was interrupted by the muttered curses of one of the warders who, having carried a sack of flour to the table for the baker, had banged his bandage-wrapped hand. The bandages immediately began to soak through red.

Seeing the filthy rag the man had wrapped around his injured hand, Judith shuddered to think what lay beneath the crude bandage. Then she knew what it was she could contribute to this house that had accepted her as one of their own. Medicine—at least a rudimentary kind of medical care. Simplistic it would be, depending entirely upon what she knew about the healing properties of various plants, mould and fungus. But with her knowledge of botany and simple cleanliness, perhaps she could make a significant difference to these people.

Stepping up to the man, Judith took his injured hand in hers.

"Would you allow me to see to your injury?"

Aghast, the man snatched his cloth hat from his head, stared steadfastly at his own feet and stepped as far back from Judith as he could without pulling his hand from her grasp, which he dared not do. It was unheard of for a woman of her noble station as the young Lord's bride-to-be, to touch a man of his own low birth in such an intimate manner. He cringed, afraid of what Lord Griffon would do to him when he heard. He could only hope the young Lady Triona and Lord Griffon's own guard would witness in his favor. As the man shot desperate glances at his fellows from the corners of his eyes, he mumbled an unintelligible response, all the while clutching his hat to his breast and shifting from foot to foot.

Taking that as a 'yes', Judith began to pick the filthy rags from his hand and issue orders.

"I will require boiling water and a deep basin, clean, freshly laundered strips of cloth and, if you have it, several slices of moldy bread."

"Judith, what do you here? Come away." Triona plucked nervously at Judith's sleeve. She did not know what to make of her friend's sudden irrational behavior and looked upon the stricken warder with pity.

Judith, on the other hand, was having trouble maintaining her resolve, now that she had actually seen the seeping, bloody bandage. As she pulled away the layers of filthy cloth the man had wound around his hand, she felt her gorge begin to rise. Stained yellow with the purulent excretion of infection, caked with dried blood, the rotting rags gave off an unholy odor. Finally, peeling away the last remaining layers, Judith held her breath to keep the noxious odor from gagging her. The offending bandages were removed and several of those surrounding them let out their collectively held breath. Judith inspected the wound closely, finding it serious but, thankfully, not so bad as she might have imagined. The flesh was severely torn, and infection had indeed set in, however, gangrene had not yet taken hold.

"You are fortunate, you might have lost your hand to gangrene if you were to continue to treat this injury as you have."

Judith was puzzled by the man's obvious discomfort, not because she handled his injured hand roughly, but by her presence. Seeing the man was embarrassed and uneasy with her speaking to him and touching him this way, Judith cast about for a way make him understand what she wanted him to do. She turned to Triona for help and had an idea.

"Triona, notice how the torn flesh has begun to whiten here about the edges and this fierce dark redness there. That is infection, which is preventing the flesh from healing and causing it to die. This infection will soon poison him if not treated properly."

She could see that all, including the injured warder, were paying attention to what she was saying. She had deliberately diverted their attention to Triona and the warder's injured hand, and therefore, away from the frantic man himself. They were listening to her, not worrying about her doing something she should not.

As she soaked the man's hand in the basin of hot water, testing it first to determine it was not too hot, she explained to him, under the pretext of explaining to Triona, the necessity of keeping the wound clean and changing the bandages daily for clean ones.

The wound now clean, Judith picked through the moldy bread, which had been fetched for her. Not finding what she needed there, she took a small bit of fine linen from the clean cloths which had been brought to her and quickly wrapped the injury. If only she had some simple medicines, penicillin... *I'm a botanist, I know what plants and herbs contain medicinal properties. It should be a simple matter to gather the items I need and adapt them to a usable form.*

"Now," addressing the man directly, "you must clean this wound daily and change this dressing. Agreed?"

The man nodded and pulled his forelock, then escaped through the arch leading to the outside stair.

"Right, if you would not mind, Cook, I would have you keep some of the moldy bread until I have seen it first. Come Triona, we still have that adventure you promised me, and I would like to explore the woods for the plants and herbs I will be needing."

She did not hear the buzz of whispered conversation from the now closely gathered scullery help, nor did she see the knowing looks and nods, the excited glances, which passed between the women of the kitchen. She did not hear the whispered, *femina saga*, wise woman, which rippled through the gathered peasantry.

Triona and their guard followed Judith meekly out of the castle. There was much to discuss with Boann later Triona thought as she listened as her friend spoke with animation about the plants she must find and where they might locate them.

Eleven

In their morning explorations, Judith and Triona, followed closely by their armed shadow, had combed the surrounding forest and meadows for plants and wild herbs that would be useful to Judith. Her script contained, at present; willow bark, from which she could extract salicin to produce a form of aspirin; the leaves of the Foxglove, which contained digitalis for treatment of heart ailments; and Sweat Woodruff, which when simmered in a mixture of wine, strawberries and honey, would act as a antioxidant for the blood. These were only simple home remedies, however, they had been proven in laboratory experiments to work. These were only a few of the 'medicaments' Judith remembered from her university days. She must remember to speak to Griffon or his father about a small place in the walled garden she had noticed next to the Keep. It would take time to locate the plants she would need and transplant some of them to a place where she could cultivate them, eventually creating a pharmacopoeia within the castle walls.

But that was for later. For now the two young women were enjoying a paddle in a shallow part of the river. The guard, as usual, was close, but with his back to them, keeping vigil. Judith and Triona, their long skirts kilted well above their knees to keep them dry, were laughing and splashing water at each other. The day had proven unusually hot and this was one way to stay cool.

The sound of a rapidly approaching horse brought the girls out of the water and caused the guard to draw his sword, prepared to defend his two charges. The man sheathed his sword as he recognized his master's approach. Griffon's horse drew down steadily upon them. He slowed only slightly, leaned down, and swept Judith up to set her before him, then urged Lugh back into a gallop. She clung to him to keep herself from being thrown from the horse. Fear effectively silenced her. The questions that came to her mind scattered like so many leaves before a storm. The only conscious thought was how an animal as imposing as Lugh could move so swiftly... and what would happen to her should she slip from his back beneath those pounding hooves.

The path they followed took them further up the river until finally Griffon slowed Lugh's pace as they approached a quiet spot. Dropping Judith to the ground, he pointed to a rocky outcropping, telling her to sit. He paced silently, his face a livid mask of fury. He would stop occasionally as if to speak, then turn his back to her to pace the forest floor again.

Judith was at first confused and she searched her memory in vain for what might have caused Griffon to be so angry. Perhaps it was as Triona had said earlier, that she should not have taken the warder's hand in the kitchen that morning, even though her intention has been to help the man. She had been told that it was not proper for a lady to become familiar with the servants, especially the male servants. Her actions seemed such a small thing to her. Then she became angry as he paced back and forth, refusing to speak or even look at her. How dare he treat her like some errant child!

Finally, his rage somewhat under control, Griffon pulled Judith to her feet.

"You shame me already, woman. We are not yet married and you bring dishonor to my name."

"I don't know what you mean. Why are you so angry with me? Griffon please, won't you tell me what I've done to make you so angry? Is it because I cleaned the warder's wounded hand this morning? Is that why you are so angry? Griffon, please, tell me what I have done."

"Do not think to confuse with guileless looks and innocent protestations. I care not of what occurred this morning. All those who were present have gone out of the way of their day's work to tell me of the innocence of your actions and how your only concern was for the warder's injury. No, no, the entire household of servants speak of nothing else but the kindness of the Lady Judith and how she would lend her healing arts to help the poor and miserable as quickly as the nobility, risking her husband's wrath. My chest was swelled with pride that my chosen wife would so quickly capture the devotion of the people that they would risk themselves to come before me to ascribe you blameless."

"Then what! What have I done to bring you pounding down upon me like some wraith from hell, snorting and steaming, all red in the face?" Judith had become angry herself. Fists clenched, she prepared to face him down.

"Oh, Etaine tried to warn me, but I would not listen. My eyes were blinded to your true nature, seeing only the innocent face, hearing only the call of my body for yours."

"I don't understand..."

"Do not speak lies to me! I saw you. In truth, every one of my men saw as you displayed yourself to them. On the small hill just the other side of the river. Hearing my men speak of two young nymphs playing in the river, I went to see for myself. There I saw as you lifted your skirts for them. Displaying for all to see what is mine." Judith suddenly realized what was going on, all of the clues fell into place, it became clear that this man that she loved unconditionally was possessed of a dark, unreasoning jealousy. Her anger dropped away as quickly as it had come upon her.

"Griffon, it was hot and we just wanted to cool off. I had your sister with me, she will tell you nothing was wrong with what we did. I kilted my skirt only to keep it dry." She raised her hand to touch his cheek, but he drew away from her touch like a petulant child.

What could possibly have happened to cause such pain that Griffon would mistrust so easily? Since first meeting this man, Judith had come to see him as possessing a great strength, capable of tremendous bravery and heroism, but also capable of being gentle and kind. Someone she could lean on, who would always protect her. Now she realized there was another side to Griffon, an injured side that needed to be held and protected as well.

"I would never do anything to intentionally hurt you. Don't you know by now that I love you? I am not being forced to marry you. You asked me and I told you that I wish to be married to you."

Sitting heavily, he hid his face behind his massive hands, as he scrubbed vigorously at his face.

Keeping his head bowed, he took her hand, "I beg your forgiveness, Lady. I have accused you unjustly. I have allowed this black jealousy to consume me. My father warned me of this."

"Of course I forgive you. I don't care about that, I care only about you. Tell me what, or who it is that has hurt you so that you would so easily mistrust me."

"Yes, it is only right that you should know." Drawing a deep breath, Griffon continued. "My first wife was Maeve. She was a young girl of fourteen years when she was given to me. It was not a love match, but arranged between my father and hers, Muiragh, with whom I had been fostered. The match was meant to strengthen our two houses. In spite of the lack of feeling between us, we seemed well enough suited to each other. However, after two miscarriages, Maeve became silent and withdrawn, but also subject to black rages and tantrums. After awhile, Maeve was got with child a third time. The pregnancy took, though it was a difficult one for her. She was kept to her bed and away from me through most of her term. When Maeve was brought to child bed, I am told it was very difficult for her, she cried out in anger at me, the birth did not go well and she did not survive it."

Griffon raised his head to look Judith in the eye. His face twisted with the pain of memories still too raw and intense, "Almost immediately, I began to hear stories of infidelity. Rumors that perhaps the child was not even mine. For three years now, I have fought with this demon."

An overpowering feeling came to her as she took him into her arms. Cradling his head against her breast, Judith tried her best to console him, murmuring soft words of love and comfort. Griffon clung to her as a drowning man clings to whatever will keep him afloat.

What a wondrous thing is the comfort of your woman's arms. Griffon felt that deep, dark part of him that he had held locked away begin to loosen ever so slightly. *Was it possible that a man could love and trust his woman? Was it an uncompromising fact that the deeper the love, the more urgent the need to feel trust and therefore the easier it became to see deception were there was none? Was mistrust a natural consequence of love?* It was something to ponder.

The high emotion of their encounter began to wane and Griffon's thoughts turned to the soft, voluptuous body of the woman he held in his arms. The softness of her breasts against his cheek drove thoughts of Maeve far back into the recess of his mind. *By the Gods, how is it this woman could bring his blood to boil with but a touch?* No, a touch was not needed, she had but to look at him in that way she had, to reduce him to a sweating, rutting bull. His hands explored the sweet swell of her buttocks, the small of her back through the fine linen of her gown. A look passed between them. Judith pushed gently away from him.

Reaching for her to pull her back to him, Griffon was stopped by the mischief in the smile that played across her lips. *What game is this?* His thought was interrupted by Judith seizing the hem of her gown and ever so slowly lifting it. First an ankle, then her calf appeared. These he had seen. The truth be known, he had bedded many women and the naked female form was by no means new to him. Yet he was spellbound, entranced as two well formed knees appeared, first one then the other. The thighs appeared next, though slowly, inch by agonizing inch...

Though her actions were deliberate and sensual, Judith was unsure of herself and more than a little nervous. But one look at Griffon's face restored the confidence in herself that her brief encounter with the now nearly forgotten Peter had all but destroyed. Her gown cascading like a breechclout between her legs and hiking her skirts a little higher, she turned one hip just so, allowing just the beginning swell of buttock to show. So intent was Griffon on the display of bare legs and hidden pleasures, when she suddenly let the hem of her skirt drop back to the ground, the disappointment was a profound thing. That is, until she reached for the laces that gathered the gown at her shoulders, tugging at them to loosen the knot. Griffin rose, pulling gently at the loosened gown, he let it drop to the ground and Judith now stood naked before him.

Judith felt her earlier bravado seep away. Her track record with men was not good. This was no twentieth century university professor that she could walk away from after kneeing him in the groin. This was a very powerful man of great strength and extreme emotions. He also stirred in her feelings that she had only read about and, until now, had begun to suspect only existed in novels. She was not sure that she would be able to control what she had set in motion here today.

To Griffon, Judith's naked form was far more beautiful than he had anticipated. Their earlier encounters had been brief and though little had been left to the imagination, there had always been that thin film of cloth that covered what now was offered freely to him. That Judith was uneasy and fearful was obvious. Her timidity touched him. The teasing way she revealed herself to him, from a more knowing woman, would have been lewd and somehow not so sensual, merely base and crude.

Reaching out hesitantly, he gently cupped one smooth, full breast in his palm. Her flesh scorched his hand and her image was forever seared upon his brain. Lifting her into his arms, Griffon carried her deeper into the forest.

Twelve

Judith lay within the protective circle of Griffon's arms, her face pressed against his chest, her legs and his entwined, she inhaled his scent deeply. She whispered softly into his chest, "Only you, My Lord, my love", then dropped into a twilight of contentment somewhere between sleep and wakefulness.

Griffon watched her as she drowsed so near sleep, remembering the last time he had done so, only days previous, on that morning he had found her at the well. How he had wanted even then, to touch her, make love to her. But to find her a virgin! If she had been ugly, with harelip or walleyed, as was so often the case in this time, perhaps he would have expected it. But a woman of her age and beauty, and a married woman as well. It had not occurred to him that she might be untouched, inexperienced. *Why did you not tell me cailín? This could have waited*, he thought, *it is no small thing to keep myself from you, but I could have waited for a time and place more suitable for your first.*

But then, perhaps this place is more appropriate, it being so like that place I did find you. Absently stroking her leg slung casually across his own, Griffon's fingers again touched the small strawberry shaped birthmark he had found on his earlier explorations. A mischievous thought flashed into his mind. Acting upon this sudden impulse, Griffon bent his head to kiss the bright red mark, then touched his tongue to it, wondering briefly if it would taste of that fruit it so cleverly imitated. His lips and tongue, as if of their own mind, began to explore the mounds and valleys they encountered there. The heavy musk of her exploded in his mind like strong drink, momentarily driving thought from his mind.

Her fingers entangled themselves in his long black hair; she had awakened. With her hands she sought to guide him, urging him on. But Griffon held back, there was no hurry this time. Pleasure could be given as well as taken. Nibbling gently at the soft flesh of the inner thigh, tasting and probing the pliable flesh, he felt her muscles become rigid. Her breath quickened, telling of her urgency as he deliberately prolonged the pleasure, holding himself away from that which he longed so desperately to taste.

Reacting mindlessly to Griffon's touch, Judith's thighs spread wide of their own accord, her fingers tangled in his hair, urging him against her trying to guide him without really knowing what it was she wanted. Her pelvis began to push against him, her back arched, and perspiration bathed her skin. Her cries spoke to him her frustration, the urgency of her need. Still, he held himself back from that ultimate kiss. Instead, his mouth teased, probing gently that spot at the top of her inner thigh, his breath whispered across her silken mound; stirring that tightly curled silk, tongue flickering, barely touching, and teasing unmercifully. His timing perfect, Griffon put his mouth on her, sending her over the edge. Her hands clenched tightly in his hair and she writhed against him, calling his name repeatedly.

Just as the storm began to abate, Griffon rose and entered her swiftly, sending Judith over the edge again, bucking, and heaving beneath him as he sent her into climax after climax...

Shuddering and bathed in perspiration, Judith slowly began to recover. Opening her eyes, she found Griffon staring intently at her. Her fingers were still tangled in his long dark hair and she let them drop to her side. Griffon rose to a sitting position, Judith still held tightly against his chest, her legs wound around his waist.

"So, my Lady," he said, using a most serious tone, "it seems you have deceived me. If you be a married woman, it would be in name only."

Judith's embarrassment was acute, as she realized that Griffon now knew that her husband had not desired her enough to consummate their marriage.

"Peter did not want me for a wife," She explained. "He wanted only someone to manage and decorate his home." Would he now reject her as Peter had? Knowing that she was unwanted even by the man to whom she had given herself in marriage, would Griffon now see her as somehow less desirable?

Gathering her into his arms, Griffon replied, "So, the Goddess has kept you for me alone." Nuzzling the nape of Judith's neck, he asked, "Now that you have tasted the pleasures of marriage, would you have more?"

Judith wrapped her arms about his neck, brought her lips to his, and gave her answer without words.

Knowing where this would inevitable lead, Griffon pulled back, "It grows late, we must return." Unwilling to leave the indulgences of pleasure she had only just discovered, Judith lay back and, watching Griffon dress, she stretched like a cat in the sun. He had no sooner donned breeches and boots when there came the noise of a horse approaching.

"Judith" he called softly. Looking around for her clothing, he remembered they had been left back at the clearing by the river.

"Wrap yourself in my cloak, someone approaches."

Without a word, Judith obeyed, creeping into a small niche in a rocky overhang where Griffon pointed. Sword in hand, he prepared to meet those who approached. His horse was in the clearing; he would have no choice but to fight. Judith was reminded all too clearly of their encounter with the thieves in the forest. Dream or reality, Judith reflected that she was continually being thrown into confusion by the sudden changes this world was constantly hurling at her.

The sound of Triona's hallo brought relief to them both, followed closely by embarrassment at their obvious state of undress.

"Sister-in-law, you really should be more careful where you leave your linens." Dangling Judith's gown from one hand, she pretended to cover her eyes with the other in mock embarrassment at her brother's bare chest.

"Really, Griffon, do cover that manly chest else I should swoon. And, I assure you, you do not need the broad sword to deal with me." The flat side of which Griffon promptly used to swat his teasing sister.

"Yon guard and I waited ever long for you to return and when you did not, we feared you might have killed each other and came to see. Your guard did blush furiously at finding Judith's clothing and would not search further into the woods for fear he would intrude."

"You, on the other hand, dear little sister, thought you might see something you should not know of until your own marriage bed."

Judith had quickly dressed while watching the playful exchange.

Taking his sister to one side, Griffon spoke softly to her, "You will hold that wagging tongue, Triona, I will not have Judith's name dishonored by you carrying tales."

"You need have no fear from me, though that guard of yours may require speaking to."

Interrupting the two siblings, Judith interjected, "I, for one, am hungry. You two may chatter back and forth, but I am for home and food. Feed me, my Lord."

Griffon threw back his head and laughed, lifting his wife-to-be into his arms and spinning her 'round.

"A woman with an appetite, by the Gods, I am blessed. And one who knows how to feed her husband, as well."

Griffon's outrageous leer brought bright pink to Judith's cheek. Though she was not so embarrassed that it stopped her from wrapping her arms about his neck, her lips meeting his in a kiss that was first gentle then quickly became that deep, soul-hunger satisfying kiss that would leave one weak-kneed. Triona watched in shocked silence at her brother's transformation. She had known three years of Griffon's dark brooding moods. This laughing, joking brother was a stranger to her—a welcome stranger.

With Triona seated on the back of the guard's horse and Judith where she preferred to be, seated before Griffon and held fast within his arms, the four of them rode back to the castle. Snuggled in close to her soon-to-be husband's chest, she sent a silent prayer to Danu. *Please, oh please, let this be real, don't let this be a dream.*

"Has it truly been just four days since first I found you?" Griffon seemed to speak the words even as Judith thought them. Soon the walls of Dun Tirlough loomed before them.

"I feel as though this is where I have always been, and was always meant to be." Judith touched Griffon's face then pulled him close for a final kiss before entering the curtain wall.

"Careful, Lady, my lust seems to arouse easily of late." He growled into her neck, tasting the salty sweetness of her skin after their afternoon of lovemaking.

Shouts of welcome from the wall roused them both.

The two lovers crossed the outer bailey and entered the inner ward, laughing, touching, very aware of skin touching skin, unconscious of watching eyes. Indeed everyone in the outer bailey as well as the inner ward stopped what activity they were at in order to watch as they passed. Judith's head was thrown back against Griffon's shoulder so she could gaze up at him as he spoke to her. The look on her face told the story to all who saw. Any who cared to look would see that Griffon, as well, adored and coveted his new bride-to-be. Though in truth, they were supposed to be husband and wife in name only as yet, it was plain to all that this was a love-match. Although, among those who watched, not all wished the young lovers well.

Thirteen

"Brother! Griffon!" A shout of greeting met them as they approached the Keep. An attractive young man, quite tall and very fair, bounded down the steps to meet them. Griffon shouted an excited greeting of his own.

"Rauen! What good fortune brings you to Dun Tirlough? How goes it with your father, my foster father? It is good you are here." The men embraced, pounding each other across the back.

"What brings me? I hear news that my foster brother, indeed, once brother-in-law, is to take a new wife. The vates tell of how young Griffon mac Connault slew two score of men, including the lady's own husband, in order that he might win the beautiful Lady Judith for his own. Do you think I would not come to see this for myself? And this vision must be the Lady Judith. I am struck dumb."

"Rauen mac Muiragh speechless? That would be welcome, though I doubt it much. This is my Lady, Judith, though the vate exaggerates in the telling of the tale, he does indeed tell the truth of my Lady's great beauty."

Having only just this morning witnessed Griffon's capacity for jealousy, Judith hung back, extending her hand and withdrawing it quickly. But Rauen was not to be put off. Lifting her from her feet, he planted a kiss soundly upon her lips. Griffon's hand strayed to his sword; half withdrew it. A dark scowl marked his face. Rauen did not notice.

"Sister, you are welcome. Though, what should induce one so fair to wed this ugly beast, I know not. Shall I champion you? Are you forced to this end? Would you have me challenge this claim? Just speak it and it shall be done." Rauen's teasing fell on deaf ears. Judith was terrified Griffon would draw upon his friend. Griffon was beyond hearing as he tried to control his rage. Only Triona, who had slipped quietly from the back of the guard's horse to join them upon the castle steps, acted quickly enough to avert disaster. Stepping between them, she deftly maneuvered Rauen by the arm and guided him up the steps.

"Master Rauen, how does your Lady Mother? Have you news to share? My mother shall be pleased to hear of the happenings in your country."

As they moved up the steps toward the castle Keep, Rauen cast a baffled look over his shoulder, only just becoming aware of his friends anger.

Judith was quick to speak. "Griffon, he meant nothing by his words."

"I know this and still I can not abide another man to touch you, or to speak words of love to you, even in jest. You will not speak to Rauen, nor be alone in his company." Griffon announced with the petulance of a child.

"If that will please you, I will do as you ask. Come, walk with me in the orchard." Linking her arm in his, Judith and Griffon made their way to the small walled orchard located between the castle and the bailey wall.

~ * ~

Elsewhere in the castle Keep, flickering candlelight and the glow of coals in the brazier did little to warm the dank clime of the lower depths of the Druid Tower.

Etaine abandoned the rage that had so quickly overcome her. It did little to further the attainment of her goals and her father, Mog Ruath, had become quite agitated by her outburst. That would not do.

"Father, I beg you forgive this unworthy child's small tantrum." She lay her head against the old man's thin shoulder and peered out over her father's shoulder. The rage that had disappeared from her countenance was there still, in the eyes, now white hot and controlled. Idly she touched the glainnader suspended by heavy chain about Mog's neck, the crystal glowed faintly at her touch.

"You know I have long desired Griffon, since the death of Ciran, my own betrothed. For propriety sake, I could do naught while his wife lived. Three years now I have waited for him to mourn. And for myself to gain the skills in the Druid arts those of the Isle of Women could impart to me. I return to find this usurper has claimed my due and my own father has sanctioned it. Father, I am undone!"

"Now, now, child. All is not lost, there is still the challenge, and the lady's husband may arrive to claim her or perhaps another with which she has had consort. Much can happen in the span of a fortnight. Besides, there is naught I could do, it is the law and young Lord Griffon's right." Patting his child's shoulder, Mog tried to comfort his distraught daughter.

Eyes dancing with a malicious glow, sudden plans forming within her devious mind, Etaine allowed the old fool to coo and cluck as he would, making her leave from him as soon as was proper.

~ * ~

In the far right corner of the Inner Ward, connected to the Great Keep and its four towers only by the low wall of the family garden, sat a low stone structure. The raw, clean surfaces of the stone attest to the newness of the building, for it had only recently been added to the ward. It is the Christian chapel of Father Adolphus. The building of the new structure came at the insistence of Bryon, one of the few impositions of his will the man had managed. Father Adolphus, while pleased with his new chapel, was not happy with its proximity to the Druid Tower. Nor was he pleased with the soon-to-be wife of the young Lord.

"Lord Bryon, is there naught can be done to stop this abomination of God's holy state? You are to be Lord of this land, you are your father's heir, would you not stop this?" Wringing his bony hands and casting eyes to heaven, Adolphus' gesticulations would be deemed comic were his audience of a less religious inclination. Even so, he was finding it difficult to maintain Bryon's attention. Adolphus was extremely grateful to have such a pious Lord as his patron. Indeed, the man had had intentions toward the brotherhood until his circumstances had changed with the death of two older brothers, leaving him as heir and future leader of this clan. However, there were times when the old cleric found Bryon a bit faye and often trying. His attention would often wander into thoughts of his own; of a suitably religious nature he had no doubt, however; dragging those thoughts back to the here and now was often difficult at best.

His wife, Annu, on the other hand, could not be more attentive. It was small compensation. The girl, devout she may be, had little or no influence with her husband's kin, and Adolphus found her to be silent and unimaginative. Adolphus dismissed her from his thoughts, turning back to Bryon.

"The Holy Scripture tells us that we shall not suffer the witch to live among us. Lord Bryon, if something is not done, we are lost."

Desperate to maintain his tenuous hold upon the man's ever-wavering attention, Adolphus continued to pressure Bryon. He dredged up every reference to witches within his arsenal of religious dogma. Rousing himself, Bryon addressed his wife.

"Annu, this is not fit conversation for one in your delicate condition. Perhaps you should seek the company of the ladies at their tapestries." Like a silent wraith, Annu rose and obediently left them.

~ * ~

In the small orchard at the opposite end of the Inner Ward, Griffon's good humor had returned. Judith's presence always seemed to lighten his mood. Sitting in the orchard on a bench against the wall of the smaller, west tower—known as the stair tower—Judith's interest had turned to tales of the Eman Macha.

"Were you also at the battle of Cuailnge?"

"Aye, we were all there, my Lord Father, Ciran and Lomnae, and myself. Bryon was not there, he was for the church. Connault felt it wise for our clan to have council with this Christian religion. The battle had gone well, the men of the Ulaid had pushed the Eman Macha back to Armagh where they suddenly rallied and regrouped. A small group of us were quickly surrounded and found ourselves cut off from the main body. Ciran and Lomnae had stayed close by Connault so they might protect him, though in truth the old Lord was still a fierce warrior. I had become separated from them. I heard my father's sluaghghairm, his war cry, and made my way to his side. Lomnae had been struck down. Connault lifted Lomnae in his arms while Ciran protected his flank and I his front. As we withdrew, Ciran too was felled. I carried him upon my shoulder trying to protect my father's back that he also would not be struck down. Lomnae was dead before ever father had taken him up. Ciran lingered many days. Then he too passed. If I had stayed with them, mayhap it would not have happened. I blame myself."

This last was said as a matter-of-fact, not as a plea for pity. It touched her heart to hear him blame himself for his brothers' deaths.

"Forgive me for recalling these painful memories." Circling her arms around his neck, she kissed his cheek.

"It is done and passed. Not forgotten, but the pain eases."

An uncomfortable silence followed. Judith knew she had evoked memories that Griffon would as soon forget.

"What is this here?" Judith had been running her fingers along the stone face of the tower and had come across something carved into the stone.

"It is nothing, just the bored mischief of a small boy."

It was a small carving of the mythical Gryphon. The very one she herself would find over a millennium later.

"You did this? As a child?"

"Aye, and received a sore backside for my trouble. Are you hungry? I will fetch you a treat."

With that he bounded up, quickly climbing a plum tree, reaching for the largest and plumpest. Jumping to her feet, Judith clapped her hands in delight as Griffon leaped to the ground, sweeping a graceful bow, holding the prize before him. He glanced briefly up and seemed to turn to stone.

"Judith! Come here to me, *now!*" he commanded.

Judith was stunned by the lightening change in his manner but did not hesitate. She moved quickly toward him, to be jerked from her feet as he took her arm and pulled her the rest of the way. That instant, an immense stone hurled to the ground, smashing the bench where they had been sitting and imbedding itself in the very spot where, only seconds before, she had stood. She would most certainly have been crushed if Griffon had not glanced up and seen the stone as it was being pushed from the tower parapet. The one thing he had not seen was the hand that shoved the stone over the edge.

Calling to his man just outside the garden wall to guard Judith, Griffon drew his sword and entered the tower only to encounter Boann, Triona, and Rauen descending the stair.

"Quickly, did you meet anyone on the stair just now, coming from the tower parapet?"

"Griffon, what has happened? No, there was no one. What is it?" Shaking off his sister's arm and her questions, Griffon turned to Rauen.

"An assassin has just now made attempt at murder. Only by the grace of the Goddess is she alive."

"Judith! I would see to her, Griffon, where is she?"

"There, mother, in the orchard, where she is guarded. Rauen, will you accompany me to the parapets?" There was no need to ask; Rauen had already drawn sword and was prepared to follow Griffon to the tower roof.

The roof was deserted when they reached it, and they had encountered no one along the way. However, they did find pry marks all round the hole in the parapet where the stone, now laying atop a shattered bench in the orchard garden below, had once been. There was no doubt, someone had deliberately pushed that stone from the tower roof.

"Indeed, Griffon, it would appear there is an assassin among us." Griffon and Rauen had returned to the garden where they had revealed to those gathered what they had discovered on the tower roof.

Griffon and Rauen had found Boann and Connault present in the orchard garden when they returned from the investigation of the tower. Judith was finding it very difficult to believe an assassin had made an attempt on her life. "No, it is not possible. I have been here at Dun Tirlough only three days. Who could possibly wish to harm me?"

"The evidence is plain. Rauen will verify it, the stone was pried loose and pushed over."

"It is true, the marks bear it out. Your life is in danger, Judith."

"Well, I don't care. Even if it is true, which I still do not believe, I will not shut myself away from the world because of it." With a toss of her long black hair, she marched into the castle, dragging Triona along behind her.

Under his breath, Griffon muttered. "The choice is not yours to make, my love."

When Boann joined Judith and Triona in their bedchambers, she found Judith sitting in the small stone embrasure, staring out at the sea, knees to chest, arms wound tightly about them. She trembled uncontrollably; the brave words spoken in the garden below were forgotten. The normally cool and austere Boann was heartsick to see the child in such a state, and gathered her into her arms to comfort her.

"There, there, child. Now that the danger is known, you will be protected. It will be seen to, do not fear." Pressing her cheek to the shining dark head, she realized that this girl, in three short days, had become as her own child to her. Boann, too had been shaken by the attack on Judith's life and how close they had come to losing her.

"Come here, Triona, do not stand there shifting from foot to foot." Making room for her on the stone bench within the narrow niche, Boann gathered her into her arms as well. The three of them sat huddled together, that small sun allowed through the slit of the loop opening warmed them little as they clung to each other.

Fourteen

A shadow figure moved silently, effortlessly through the midnight forest. No moon lit the figure's path, yet there was no hesitation. A highly polished silver bowl was held before the mute form. The bowl was made of the purest silver, the sides etched over in the curvilinear style, the intersecting circular patterns covered most of the surface, and handles at each side were attached with ornately enameled escutcheons. A bronze dagger balanced across the lip of the bowl. The dagger was of a ritual nature and was itself ornately decorated, delicately etched in swirling circular patterns, giving strength through the power of three. Three circles within a circle of three repeated again and again. The dagger's shaft fit neatly into the handgrip that, upon close observation, was the gaping mouth of the Goddess, from which the shaft emerged. The bowl and dagger were carried with great care given as not to spill the contents.

The figure paused beneath the wide spread arms of a mighty oak, the limbs dripped curtains of mistletoe. Seemingly satisfied with the spot, she, for the figure was most definitely a she, waited patiently. Her wait was not long. Soon the heavy clouds broke open, and the moon shone brightly through the hole found there. The light would not last long so the silent figure moved quickly, and stepped into the shaft of moonlight. Circling opposite to the rotation of the sun, she described upon the blanket of moss at her feet a magical ring using the sacred water she carried in the bowl; once, twice, three times round. Carefully setting the bowl at her feet, she gazed intently into the water remaining. She then passed the dagger over the bowl; again, once, twice, three times. Pressing the tip of the dagger's blade against her finger, blood was drawn and three drops allowed to fall onto the surface of the water.

"Speak, Mother. What is't this auld one must see?" Turning her face upward, the light from the waning moon shone briefly on her face...

Judith woke with a start. Again, she'd dreamt of the old woman from the forest. What could it mean? A warning?

~ * ~

The grooms touched their forelocks and ducked their heads as Griffon and Judith passed by, the craftsmen stood at their doors to watch the couple pass. The guardsmen of the outer bailey called greetings as Griffon and Judith passed through the gate, each mounted on their own horse; Griffon on Lugh, Judith on a small pony, much to her chagrin. She had come to enjoy her accustomed spot, seated before Griffon on Lugh's broad back.

Griffon turned their mounts not toward the forest but to the cliff top, which they followed for some distance. The cliff rose high above the sea; the breeze carried the smell and taste of it to them. The day was clear and brilliant, though the sea mists could be seen to gather far off the coast, obscuring the already hazy line of that land of Picts called Caledonia.

The invigorating feel and smell of the ocean made their spirits run high. Judith, especially, seemed full of devilment.

"My Lord, do you not find it warm wearing all that heavy leather?" Judith smiled, eyes wide with innocence. Griffon seemed not to take her meaning, perhaps something more direct was needed.

"I fear the wool of this gown is entirely too warm for such a day as this, my Lord." She plucked idly at the laces of her gown. The heat and interest in his expression showed how well Griffon was reminded all too clearly of his encounter of yesterday with those very same laces and how easily they were loosed.

"This is a lovely spot, my Lord. The way the wild flowers and tall grasses grow right up to the edge of the cliff. Perhaps we could stop for while and I could help you remove some of that heavy leather and you could help me with this terribly warm gown." The look she gave him was neither coy nor innocent, but as forward as she could manage.

Laughing, Griffon replied, "My Lady, I would be most pleased to help you out of the offending gown. Unfortunately, we are on a mission and I fear that once I endeavor to remove you from this garment which provokes you so, it may require several hours of... contemplation... to come up with a suitable alternative. And, while I am always ready to pursue... contemplation... of such a nature, we have some distance to travel and now is not the best time."

Judith too laughed. She was not put off by Griffon's refusal. His occasional glances stray to where the open-sided overgown revealed her thighs with the undergown stretched tightly across them. Or there, at the bodice where the still loosened laces and the gentle motion of her mount allowed her breasts to move provocatively beneath the soft folds of the fine wool garment. No, she was not annoyed.

Presently, they came to a spot where the forest grew right up to the cliff's edge. Here Griffon turned inland, moving deep into the forest.

"Where is it we are headed? I should be with Boann, for I have much to learn from her and I told her I would help today."

"Where we are headed is a surprise. Soon enough you will have a home to run. For now we will enjoy what freedom we have."

The ocean mists had moved to the coast and begun to insinuate itself through the forest trees, swirling about the horses' feet. Seeking protection from the damp and drawing her cloak close about her, a small sigh escapes her lips.

"What sigh is this? A heavy heart, a desire unfulfilled? You are disappointed with me as I have not performed my husbandly duty."

"Disappointed? No! Contented. Pleased. Can we travel like this forever, Griffon? I want it never to end."

"Your backside would be uncommon sore after but a short time."

"Only in reality. In fantasy, we would spend our days riding the forests, seeking adventure. Occasionally you would fight off a dragon or marauding cutthroats. The nights we would spend making love under the stars. Is this not my dream? Perhaps, if I concentrate very hard, I can make it so."

"A fantasy indeed. One I would gladly share with you, however, we have arrived."

At first, Judith saw nothing except towering conifers filtering the sun to a narrow gloom. A rocky outcropping of granite rose from the forest floor straight up near as high as the treetops. Not a sheer cliff, but one whose surface was molded by time. Mossy ledges and deep crevasses from which fern and small trees grew created a vertical landscape on this granite face.

As her eyes adjusted to the gloom of the forest, she began to make out the shape of a tiny stone hut, well hidden within the shadow of the cliff. There appeared at the doorway a stooped and gnarled figure. Black eyes shone out from a weathered, nut-brown face. Long gray hair hung in a thick rope. The tiny figure appeared to be as much a part of the forest as the trees themselves and perhaps as ancient. It was the same old woman of her dreams. As Griffon helped Judith down from her horse, the elderly fairy approached them calling out to Griffon.

"Griffon, do thee come child?" she said in a voice that belied the age of the speaker.

"Yes, auld mother, it is I. I have brought someone I would present to you."

"Judith, I would have you meet Aguaine, who is priestess to the Mother Goddess Danu, also, mother to Boann and Granddame to me. Aguaine, this is the Lady, Judith, who is to be my bride."

Sharp black eyes inspected Judith from head to foot. Though Judith herself was small, this woman came barely above her shoulder. Gnarled brown fingers reached out to poke, tug at locks of hair and finger fabric. Not a word did she speak during this inspection as she circled Judith like a buyer at a cattle sale. She cackled gleefully as she measured Judith's pelvis with the spread of her hands.

Beneath her breath, she murmured "It is well thee have done, Mother Danu."

Aloud she said, "At least thee'll no lose this one to child birth. Unlike that one thee first did wed, this one is built to bear babes. I would see thy teeth, girl. Good, good, healthy, too. Thee have chosen well boy. Come, sit, I would bring ale."

Stone walls formed the one room hut, one of them the cliff wall itself. Its floor was the well-swept floor of the forest. No windows relieved the gloom that gathered within, though a simple iron brazier brought warmth as well as a cheery glow. A tiny wood bench with straw mattress against one wall for sleeping, and rough-hewn table with bench was the only furniture.

It was not the simplicity of the life lived here that fascinated Judith so, but the pharmacopoeia that hung from its rafters and lined its walls.

There were herbs and plants too numerous to name, drying in bunches hung from the rafters. Judith easily spotted foxglove, which she knew was used for the treatment of the heart, leaves of the wild cherry, wolfsbane and willow bark were but a few. On the table was the root of the Lady's Slipper orchid and the cuckooflower, which Aguaine had been grinding to powder in a stone bowl. Shelves lining the walls contained pots of ointments and unguents for soothing and healing. All of these plants Judith recognized. Their value in healing was well known.

It was the others that repelled and yet drew her close. There on the table lay a staff of yew carved over with fairy faces that seemed to wink, smile, and peer out at her from behind carved leaves and vines. Dry grasses, mixed with thistles, puffballs and leaves were cleverly woven into the likeness of an armed man, a small bit of stick as broadsword, clutched in a tiny wicker fist. And there, sitting in a place of honor on a simple stone altar, in the farthest darkest corner of the tiny room, a bowl of silver, its surface etched in intersecting circular patterns, handles at each side attached with ornate enamel escutcheons. An intricately carved bronze dagger was balanced across the lip of the bowl. Of course, Judith could not see these details, but she knew that they were there.

When she looked at Aguaine, a curious expression came over the old woman's face. Light danced in the black raisin eyes. They seemed to be telling her something. She started to speak, but the look in Aguaine's eyes told her that now was not the time. She must be content to wait, the old woman would tell her in good time.

Aguaine fussed with Griffon, bringing him food and ale. She doted on her grandson and it was obvious that he loved the old woman as well. They spoke of many things; the coming marriage, the changing of the seasons in the forest. Judith found she was completely charmed by the old elf and hung on her every word.

"Why is it that you live in such a remote place? Why do you not live in the Keep with the rest of the family?"

It was Griffon who answered. "My father and my brother fear Aguaine for she is of the old race and was once a very powerful priestess of the old Gods. Now she is old and seeks the comfort of family, yet insists she must never leave the forest."

Perhaps not so old or useless, thinks Judith. The priestess' eyes confirm her thoughts; they tell Judith another story, of one whom is still very active in the affairs of her Goddess and her kin.

"Connault will not have her near him, so I have brought her here, to my land which was given to me by Brude, that I might see that she is cared for."

"Why does Connault fear you so?"

"When Boann was brought into this world, her father, Brude, did make a promise to me that she would be given in marriage to one who would preserve the old ways. The vow has been broken."

"Broken. How?"

"The Mother cares not how a deed is done, but that it has been done. Done it is and must be undone."

"I don't understand. Connault has the Druid, Mog Ruath, with him as his adviser. Doesn't that mean that the vow has been kept?"

"Pah!" Aguaine spat the word at the floor. "That old Druid has naught to do with Danu." She would have gone on, however Griffon interrupted.

"We must take our leave of you, Auld Mother, the distance we must travel is great and it will be fully dark before we reach Dun Tirlough." Griffon's discomfort at the turn of the conversation was evident.

"Go thee outside, Griffon. I would speak alone to our Judith."

"Yes, Grandmother." Kissing the leathered old cheek, Griffon obeyed her without question.

"'Thee have crossed great distance and time to come to this place which is unknown to thee and is now accepted as it is. Thee have been well chosen."

"You know? You know where, and when, I come from?"

"I have the gift of the sight. I know what is, what has been and what will be."

"How did I get here? How long will I be here? Aguaine, please tell me, I must know. Will I find happiness here only to be thrust back to where I was before?"

"Only thee can know that, child. It rests in these hands." The old woman would say no more on the subject, only patted Judith's hands which she had clasped in her own. Then she pushed Judith through the door to where Griffon waited.

"Will you at least come to Dun Tirlough when Griffon and I are to be married? I have no family here, and I have come to feel very close to you."

"Aye, I will, if old Connault will have me."

On their return to the castle, Judith wanted to know more about why the old woman was so feared by Connault and Bryon.

"When Connault was to wed Boann, Aguaine went to him and required of him a vow. Because Boann was the child of a Druid king and a priestess of the old Gods, conceived at Beltaine, she could not be given to just any man for marriage. The man who wed her must vow that he and his heirs would maintain the old ways. Connault feared that because Bryon was raised a Christian and is now to be his heir, Aguaine would consider the vow broken and would bring Danu's wrath onto him and our clan."

"But surely she can not hold the death of your brothers against Connault. She must understand the circumstances that have brought about Bryon becoming your father's heir."

"Aguaine has her own ways and speaks of them to no one. Aguaine understands that there is room for all Gods within the hearts of the people but it is this new God that will tolerate no others, indeed, would have it that no others exist. As long as the people are free to worship as they will, as long as the old rituals are preserved, Aguaine will be content."

"What will happen when Bryon gains power here and Christianity drives out the old ways?"

"It will not happen, not in her lifetime. Aguaine is safe and happy here on my land. Boann comes here to see her often. She will die in peace."

"Does that mean that once Aguaine has passed away, Connault's vow is no longer valid?"

"My father does believe in the old ways. Though he does little to recognize the old rituals, the people are free to believe as they would as long as he lives. In his heart, he knows that a vow is a vow and must be kept. I think he does believe that, with Aguaine's passing, once he himself is gone, what Bryon does is no longer his concern. I would argue that while he is alive, he must do all that he can to see that the vow is kept after his death."

"How would he do that, Griffon? You know that Bryon is a Christian and would bring Christianity to the people. Once he is Lord here, the people will become Christian whether they like it or not. Adolphus would see to that. I cannot imagine that he would ever make any promise that compromises his Christian beliefs."

"As you say, Bryon is a Christian and will always be a Christian. But, I do not believe he would force his beliefs on the people. It is Adolphus who would do this, in Bryon's name. Bryon always has been, and always will be, a reticent. He loves his books and tracts overmuch and would not often stir himself to see to the people. It is Adolphus who will rule, in action if not in name."

"And what of you and your mother and sister once Adolphus gains this power? Do you think he would try to do you harm or drive you from your father's land?"

"It is without doubt that the old cleric holds no love of myself and certain members of my family. It is doubtful he would attempt anything so forthright as banishment or physical harm. His methods are more devious. It does not matter; it would not come to that. I have my own lands, which you and I shall occupy soon after our marriage. My mother, and sister, if she has not wed, would join us there upon my father's death."

"So what is the answer, then? How does your father keep faith with Aguaine's wishes?"

"I wish the answer was within me, Judith. There is one way; though it is doubtful Connault would ever resort to this. There is a very ancient Celtic law, which is seldom invoked. This law states that any male kin, up to five times removed, may be named as heir. My father has younger brothers who still live, it would be possible to name one or other his heir."

"And what of you, Griffon? Couldn't Connault name you his heir?"

"I would not have it so. I will not have titles and land come between my brother and me. I have my own land and have no designs upon my father's, nor my brother's claim to them."

"How did you come to acquire this piece of land so close to Dun Tirlough?"

"After the battle of Cuailnge, King Brude, who was my Grandsire, took possession of the lands of Finn Mhaonaigh which, as you have seen, are located just south of Dun Tirlough. Finn had withheld men promised to Brude in hopes that he might see which way the battle would go, before committing men to battle. It is a very expensive proposition to send that many men to wage war. Finn had hoped to see who would gain the upper hand, then throw his men into support of whoever was winning at the last moment. He miscalculated and by the time he arrived, the battle was over and he found himself in disgrace. Brude lost a son and three grandsons, two of them my brothers, in that battle. He took the man's lands and his life. His wife and children were put off the land, which was given to me."

Griffon wondered at her silence.

"What troubles you?"

"What happened to them, Griffon? The wife and children of Finn Mhaonaigh?"

"Unless the lady had family to take them in, most likely they are dead."

"Dead! How awful. Couldn't you have taken them in?"

"It sounds cruel, Judith, but this is how it must be. How will a man know the consequences of his actions? Just to take a man's life for treachery he commits is not enough. Many are those who will wager their own lives. But, to know that the lives of your children are affected by your actions, this a man will understand."

Fifteen

The next morning Judith and Triona prepared to visit the forest and high meadows. Judith had it in her mind to look for more medicinal plants and herbs. Triona was just braiding Judith's hair when Boann entered the chamber.

"Judith, there is someone I feel you must meet. I fear if it were left to my son to make the introductions it would not be done."

Boann reached behind her and brought forward a child. A wee small girl with bright red braids that couldn't quite keep all of that baby fine hair under control. Wispy red-gold locks escaped and frolicked all around a tiny cherub face. Huge green eyes stared at Judith with reserve; a plump little thumb was tucked neatly into a rosebud mouth. The other hand clung to Boann's skirt, which she relinquished reluctantly as Boann pushed her gently forward.

"Mairead." Stooping to the child's height, Boann brushed at the child's unruly hair with absent fingers. "This is Lady Judith who is soon to be your father's wife and your mistress." Mairead made a small obeisance to Judith then hid her face in her grandmother's shoulder.

Judith was enchanted with the child from first glance and dropped to her knees, gathering her into her arms.

"Aren't you the most precious little girl I've ever seen?" She cooed and cuddled the child until Mairead would finally look at her.

"Are you my mother?" She asked quite solemnly.

"Yes, precious, soon I will be your mother. What do you think of that?"

Considering for a moment, her tiny features set in a slight frown, she nodded finally. "Yes, I would like that, my Lady."

Hugging the little girl to her, Judith could barely contain laughter at the child's solemn pronouncement. "Good, then you shall accompany your Aunt Triona and myself to the forest meadows. Would you like that?"

"Oh, yes! May I granddame? Please!" Jumping up and down, clapping her hands, and pulling at Boann, Mairead soon had them all laughing.

"Yes, child, go tell nurse to change you out of your good gown and into your old one." Mairead ran from the chamber, yelling for her nurse.

"She is three years old. Maeve died, but Griffon's child lived. You must know, Griffon refuses to see or speak to the child. I fear he blames her for her mother's death."

Evidently, Griffon had confided in neither his mother, nor his sister about the rumors of Maeve's infidelity.

"Perhaps now that he is to be married again, that will change. Go now, have fun, it is good of you to take the child with you, Judith."

"Not at all, she is a beautiful, perfect little angel. I don't know how anyone could not love her." She did love the child, she had captured Judith's heart just as her father had.

"Go now, I will send her to you in the courtyard."

Ten minutes later, the three of them were making their way across the outer bailey, their guard, now three strong, followed close behind the women. Griffon, who was working out with his men on the practice field, wondered at the sudden silence. He turned to watch, as had the others, as the three ladies crossed the outer bailey. One shining dark head, small and delicate, the other tall and slender with radiant red-gold hair and the tiny miniature between them, followed closely by their three silent guardians. They passed out through the barbican, out of the castle grounds. It made him seethe to find so many eyes following his young bride across the open grounds. Rauen in particular had shown great interest. Resuming their practice, Griffon struck out with his broad sword with renewed vigor, jealousy putting even greater strength behind the blows until his partner, driven to the ground, cried out for mercy. Returning sword to sheath, Griffon strode from the grounds, leaving the man where he lay still stunned by the fury behind his Lord's blows.

Although he knew most certainly that it was not an honorable thing he would do, it was Griffon's intention to follow the young women. Although he had placed guards with them, he must know for himself. Perhaps it was her intention to meet a lover, might she not have enlisted Triona to aid her? Women were a treacherous lot and often conspired together. Perhaps it was one of his own men, one of her guards she was to take as a lover. He would drive himself mad with these thoughts. Better to follow and see for himself.

He knew of their destination so it would be a small matter to ride fast and direct, to be there watching before they arrived. Boann had told him they would go to the high meadow, Clonmacconaul, the meadow of the sons of Connault.

Lomnae and Ciran had cleared the forest there just before the battle that had taken them. It had been intended to build upon the land the rath where Ciran and Etaine would live once married. The wild creatures had again reclaimed the land and it was now a meadow abundant in wild flowers and herbs. After the deaths of Ciran and Lomnae, Connault could not bring himself to build there and had named the place in memory of his two lost sons. Clonmacconaul. This is where Judith and his sister were now destined.

But why was the child with them? With his horse well hidden from the party below he seated himself and he watched as they went about their play. Griffon watched Judith as she gathered first one herb, then another, binding the ends securely so they may be strung together then hung to dry. He had watched Aguaine perform this task many times. Some she removed from the soil, roots and all, gently wrapping the root ball with small bits of damp linen.

His eyes strayed often to the child, her copper red hair catching the sunlight, so very like Triona that they could be mother and child. Mairead went often to Judith to show some prize that she had found. Whether it was a prize or not, a great show was always made over the treasure and with great ceremony, placed in a small script of her own.

A scene of great peace and contentment, Griffon was, nevertheless, well aware when Judith's search brought her close to the forest edge then into the forest itself. Now he would know whom her lover was. He would slay the man even as he lay with her. He would cut the man's still beating heart from his breast and eat the heart of his enemy as the old ones had done, drawing strength from the killing of his adversary. Griffon backed stealthily into the forest behind him, not wanting to alert those below by his movement. He circled the meadow, intending to come upon Judith with her lover, catch them in the act. She had moved much further into the forest and away from the meadow than Griffon had anticipated, though he tracked her movements easily.

But when he did come upon her, he found her not in the arms of another, but down on her hands and knees, skirt kilted up out of the dirt, intent upon something she had dug from the earth. He watched as she labored at her task. The backs of her bare thighs captivated him. Driven by his imagination, he fancied he could smell her scent on the slight breeze that stirred the forest.

She had removed the tight fitting tunic as not to soil it, so her breasts moved freely beneath the thin linen gown. Slightly damp from the exertion of her labors, the gown clung to her, outlining her slight frame. Suddenly ashamed to be spying upon his soon-to-be wife, Griffon stepped abruptly from the cover of the trees where he had watched. Startled, Judith fell back then realized it was Griffon who approached.

"You frightened me, Griffon. I thought perhaps I had wandered too far into the forest and was now to pay for it."

"You have, and you will, my Lady." Griffon thrust his still drawn sword into the ground, unbuckled the sheath, and dropped it to the ground beside it.

Judith had never been pursued so passionately and so relentlessly. No man had ever desired her so completely. It thrilled her—it frightened her. Never had she felt such power as a woman, nor been so aware of her own desires.

When he came to her, she was not the docile creature he had taken by the river the previous day. She leapt at him, knocking him to his back. Straddling him, she thrust herself onto him, taking him into her all at once. Leaning low, her nipples brushed against his chest. Attempting to pin his powerful arms to the ground with her small hands, she whispered into his ear.

"You are a great black stallion, my Lord, and I would make you my own." She flicked his ear with her tongue.

"I am yours to do with as you please, Lady." Griffon lay back, groaning as each twitch of her hips brought waves of pleasure. The fury of her passion astounded him and he gave himself over to it, met it with his own.

Spent and perspiring, Judith collapsed upon Griffon's chest. Still straddling his hips, she stroked the taught skin of his upper arms, delighting in the feel of hard muscles that lay beneath her hands. Trailing small kisses across his chest and belly, Judith began to slide down his torso; she felt his response to her touch. His fingers tangled in her thick black hair as she moved ever lower. A deep animal sound was torn from his throat as he reveled in her touch.

Griffon allowed himself just a few moments more of total abandonment to pleasure, then with enormous effort of will, bade her stop.

"We must return to the meadow. They will be searching for you, and I will have the heads of those three who have allowed you to wander into the forest alone."

"Please, Griffon, do not be too harsh with them. How else am I to be alone with you, like this, if I can not elude your guards?"

"Very well, but only if you promise to elude them only when I have instructed you where and when to do so."

"As you wish, my Lord." Performing an exaggerated obeisance, Judith stuck her tongue out at him, lifted her skirt and began to run. Griffon was caught still putting on his boot, so Judith had a good head start when he took out after her. By the time he had caught up with her, they were back at the meadow. He tackled her from behind and they fell laughing and rolling on the ground, into the clearing. They both looked up to find Rauen sitting on horseback watching them with an amused look on his face.

"Well, foster brother, I am glad to find it was not assassins or kidnappers that carried the Lady off. Your guardsmen came to fetch help when Judith turned up missing. I sent one back to the castle with Triona and Mairead, the other two are searching the woods to the east. Here they come now."

"Carried me off, indeed he did. Transformed into a magnificent black stallion, he carried me across the forest floor."

"Careful, Lady, my foster brother is an unruly beast in human form, I shudder to think of him in animal guise."

"I am but a new born kitten in these small hands," Griffon said as he kissed each palm in turn. "Now, enough of this talk, before I am completely unmanned."

The two guardsmen arrived with their horses and the three returned to the castle in a companionable manner, the two guardsmen at their rear. Judith was relieved to find that Griffon displayed no animosity toward Rauen when he spoke to her, and she in turn was careful to show no interest toward Rauen.

Sixteen

"Tell me, my son, what has agitated you so?" Father Adolphus guided the young guardsman to a nearby bench.

"I am called Hugh, Father. I have recently come to do service here as part of my father's obligation to Lord Connault."

"Yes, Hugh, I recall when you arrived. You are a good Christian boy and have not missed mass except when service to Lord Connault required. What troubles you, boy?"

"Yester morn, I was charged with guarding the ladies as they wished to collect flowers at Clonmacconaul. Strange doings occurred, Father. I must confess, I am confused in my duty and where my loyalty should lie."

"You must always remain feal to your liege Lord, my son, however, Christ demands absolute loyalty as well. Tell me what occurred and I shall judge what your path should be."

"It was her, Father, that evil one, the Lady Judith. It was not flowers she picked, but strange herbs and such. Digging roots from the ground, muttering strange words.

And the young Lord Griffon, sat upon a hill and watched. We pretended not to see but all knew he was there, even the wee child. It was shortly after, the woman disappeared. Suddenly. Vanished. And Lord Griffon also was gone from his watch."

Taking a deep breath, the boy continued.

"I went to fetch help and met Lord Rauen and returned with him. He sent Finnen back with Lady Triona and the child. The other lad and I were sent to search the woods. I was afraid, Father, I did not want to venture into the forest. Who knows what doings go on in those woods."

"What happened then, son?"

"Just as we were to enter the woods, we heard voices from the opposite side where Lord Rauen was to search. And there they were, just appeared from nowhere. I heard her say with my own ears, Father, I swear before God, I do not lie... the witch said she had turned Lord Griffon into a great black stallion and ridden him through the forest."

"What should I do, Father? Should I tell Lord Connault, the black witch has put Satan's mark on his son?"

"Lord Connault is not a Christian, Hugh, he will take no heed. I shall handle this. Bless you, boy. I know it took great courage to come to me with this."

"As you say, Father."

Father Adolphus left shortly after Hugh, to find Bryon. He had forgotten that Annu waited to confess and receive communion, her wraithlike figure all but hidden in the deep shadows of the chapel. He must find a way to shake

Bryon out of his apathy. The good people of this house must be protected. He felt it was already too late for Griffon, always a headstrong boy more given to the pagan practices anyway. The demon had made him her consort, he was now lost to Christ.

While Adolphus was busy trying to convince Bryon of Judith's guilt, Judith had tired of the company of women in the solarium. A steady stream of stories about childbirth, weaving and other domestic duties had put her nearly to sleep. Perhaps a walk in the orchard gardens. She could use the time alone to think about Griffon and his jealousy. She did not care for this feeling of being a possession that he quartered from others, she wanted him to see her as a person capable of making the decision to be faithful to him. As she wandered through the garden, Judith became aware she was not alone. There, under an ancient apple tree, stood Rauen and Triona locked in a lover's embrace. Clearing her throat discretely, she moved toward them.

"Well, Rauen, we now know the true reason for your sudden visit."

Red faced, they cast guilty glances at each other then at Judith.

"Judith," Triona pleaded. "You must not tell anyone you saw Rauen and I together. Rauen's father, though landed is not noble, and Rauen is a younger son and will not inherit. If it is known that we meet in secret, my father would be furious."

"When Triona and I last met, I felt there was cause to believe she would have me. At that time she was still too young to be wed, and I had no prospects and did not consider myself a suitable choice for a husband. I now have a position with Brennus and am able to provide for a wife, though this does not change the circumstance of my birth. It came to me that Triona had been promised a love match and I came straight away to see if the Lady was of a like mind and to press for a betrothal."

"Yes, and I believe I know her answer, after seeing you two just now. No, no, Triona, I will tell no one. But you two must tell Connault immediately."

"Hush, someone approaches. It is Etaine, she must not see me." Triona slipped quietly into the gathering shadows. Rauen and Judith also parted, each remembering Griffon's jealousy. But, Etaine's sharp eyes had missed nothing. A small disquieting smile touched perfectly formed lips.

When Judith and Triona arrived for dinner that evening, Griffon was already seated, with Etaine seated next to him. Deep in conversation, she leaned into his arm as she spoke close to his ear in low tones. Her glance at Judith was dismissive and she hurried not in the least to release Griffon's arm.

As he always did, he met her at the chamber door to escort her to her place. His jaw was set like granite, the vein in his neck jumped; his eyes were cold and angry. But he did not accuse, threaten, or even raise his voice to her. He held her arm tightly, led her to her seat, and told her in a voice as calm and cold as death to sit and eat and not to speak to him if she valued her life.

Confused and upset, Judith could not imagine what she had done to deserve this treatment. The day had been so perfect until now. Griffon's sudden mood swings kept her in continual turmoil. She nibbled at the delicacies on her plate; all thoughts of food were gone, and only sipped at the wine. Her stomach turned over at the sight of the sweetbreads someone had left by her plate. Judith would never be able to understand why bull testicles would be considered such a delicacy. Unnoticed, she slipped them, one at a time, to one of the many dogs always present at meals, hoping for just such a treat.

The rest of the meal she spent in silence with her hands in her lap, eyes cast down. Finally, ashamed of herself for her meekness, she rose from her seat with all the dignity she could summon and turned to Griffon.

"When you are ready to treat me in a civil manner, my Lord Griffon, you will find me in my chambers." Deftly avoiding Griffon's angry grasp, she excused herself and left the room. Knowing she had thrown down the gauntlet, she listened for his footsteps to follow her, and was not disappointed. She was not, however, prepared for the fury that met her when he spun her around to face him.

"You dare to shame me in my own home, in front of clansmen and servants, woman? I will tell you when you may leave and where you may go."

Judith had to stand on tiptoes to look Griffon in the face, but she managed. Her own anger had gotten the better of her.

"How dare you! I will not be treated like some piece of gold plate, which you take out and fondle when the mood suits you, only to be put away out of sight when your interest wanes. I will not stand for being treated as you treated me this evening. If you are angry with me, be man enough to face me and tell me you're angry, but do not treat me as though I do not exist. And at least have the decency to keep your dalliance with Etaine a private matter. Must you parade it before me and everyone else? It is you who shame me, not I you."

"Pretty words, Lady, but the lie still stinks. You would have me think you jealous of my friendship with Etaine, who is like a sister to me. Do you deny being in the orchard with Rauen. Do not lie, you were seen."

What could she do? Judith had promised Triona not to tell of her secret tryst with Rauen in the orchard?

"I went to the orchard because I wanted to be alone. Rauen was already there, we exchanged a word, then parted. If you must send your precious Etaine to spy on me, she could at least report the events accurately. I will not discuss this any further."

A disturbance in the dining hall distracted them. A clansman leaving from the hall was asked what had occurred.

"Two dogs found dead beneath the table, Lord Griffon. Poisoned, says Mog Ruath.

Judith's blood turned to ice, "Where beneath the table were they found, at whose place?"

"Why, just where you sat, mistress." the man replied and continued on his way. But Griffon did not notice, for all color had drained from Judith's face, her knees began to buckle. He caught her up in his arms, all anger gone.

"Judith, my love, are you ill. Shall I call Mog?"

"No, I am not ill. Sick at heart perhaps. Those dogs are dead because of me. I was upset because you were angry with me and unable to eat, so I fed my meal to the dogs. The poison was meant for me."

Setting her on a bench beside the huge fireplace, Griffon went to fetch wine.

"Sip this. Slowly."

"Griffon, what kind of fiend would try to poison me in this manner. What if I had saved those treats for Mairead? It's too awful to think of. Griffon, I'm frightened."

Holding her tightly, Griffon kissed her hair, face, eyes, and lips. All thought of jealousy, real or imagined driven, for the moment, from his thoughts at the idea of losing her.

"No harm shall ever come to you as long as I am able to prevent it. You shall be moved to the Guard Tower. Only Boann or I shall be allowed to enter. Once the period of waiting has passed and we are married, I shall take you from Dun Tirlough to my properties to the south."

"Leave here? I guess I knew we would. You have told me more than once that we would leave, but somehow I had thought this your home."

"These three years since Maeve passed, it has been. The child needed a home, I was not prepared to give her one."

"Griffon, please do not lock me away in that tower. I'll be more careful. I will keep guards with me at all times. Please, I can not be locked in that tower for two weeks."

"It has been decided. It is best for you. Guards will be posted so none but the family may enter. Go to your chambers now, Judith, I must inform Connault. It will be arranged to move your things to the Guard Tower. And do not expect Rauen to be visiting you there." Some of his old jealousy returning. He was beginning to realize this was his answer to keeping Judith from the attention of other men; he did not like himself for having these thoughts, but that did not change his mind.

"Go, do as I say. I must investigate the death of these dogs. Mog Ruath should surely know by now if poison is indeed the cause."

Making sure Judith had entered the Maiden Tower, Griffon posted a guard with instruction that Lady Judith was to be escorted to the Guard Tower and was not to be allowed to leave unless accompanied by himself or Connault.

Seventeen

Time passed slowly for Judith within the Guard Tower. No brightly colored tapestries hung from the walls to lift the spirit or warm the damp, cold interior. No cheery fire lit the small stone room, only an iron brazier, which took the chill from the air, but did little to warm the soul. The floor was bare stone, no thick reed covering to keep the chill from penetrating through her thin cloth shoes.

Only Boann was allowed to visit her and she, having duties of her own, was only occasional company. The hours hung like stones about Judith's neck. Her only real contact to the outside world was a narrow window-like opening. Through this narrow embrasure, Judith could see only a small corner of the bailey below and an even smaller fragment of the sea.

Try as she might, she could not convince herself that once their marriage was confirmed and they left Dun Tirlough, her ordeal would end. Until Griffon could put aside his jealousy and suspicion, she would continue to be under constant watch, always a prisoner in one way or another. Judith began to spend the long hours of her imprisonment drying and preparing the plants and herbs she had collected for medicine. Though her heart was not in it, the work helped the time to pass. As she prepared the Monkshood, the smallest seed of an idea began to form. Before long, it had germinated and begun to flourish.

Rumors began to circulate through the outer bailey. Lady Judith had been imprisoned by Lord Griffon to keep her from running from him, some said. All had witnessed the change in Lord Griffon when Maeve had died, now his black moods and sudden rages had become directed at his new bride, others said.

The warder, using his now healed hand as evidence, said that Lord Griffon was afraid that the Christians would burn Lady Judith as a witch and had locked her in the tower to prevent her from practicing her healing arts. The kitchen servants nodded wisely, letting it be known to all that they had witnessed Lady Judith's healing ways. She was one of the 'auld ones', they said, and Lord Connault was afraid of her, as he was afraid of Aguaine.

From the beginning, Judith had been a favorite with the guardsmen. But, loyal to their young Lord, they refused to believe the circulating rumors, including the one that said Lord Griffon had not found Judith abandoned by an uncaring husband, but had actually kidnapped her and the lady was being held against her will. They refused to listen to these wild rumors, reminding all who would listen of the two lovers who only recently had ridden through this very bailey, unmindful of all else but each other. But they could not help but wonder why the lady languished in the Guard Tower while Lord Griffon raged through the ward like a wounded lion.

Indeed, locking Judith in the Guard Tower had not brought Griffon peace as he had thought. He greatly regretted locking her away like a criminal, but even so, his jealousy toward Rauen—toward any man who would so much as look at her—grew as each day passed. His temper, never known to be overlong, shortened noticeably. Only the most brave, or foolhardy, dared to approach Lord Griffon and only for the most pressing of reasons, stating their business and hurrying from his presence lest the unfortunate messenger be caught up in the wrath of Lord Griffon. None would partner with him on the practice fields.

In the Inner Ward, within the Keep, Etaine was using Judith's incarceration to full advantage.

"Griffon, what need have you of a woman that must be kept confined to her tower to prevent her from straying?"

"Judith is being kept safe within the tower, Etaine. Twice an assassin has made attempt at her life. There will not be a third as long as I can prevent it." But even he did not believe the words he spoke.

"Do you think me a fool, Griffon? I know why she sits in the Guard Tower. For now, you can control her. But what of later? Will you have her guarded always? Can you prevent a lover from finding her? Do you not see the way she sits in her tower, staring out to sea, pining for her lover? The woman has made you a mockery in the eyes of your men, indeed, the entire outer bailey."

Griffon dismissed Etaine's words, and her, with a wave of his hand, but he could not dismiss them from his mind. He sat before the huge fireplace brooding over her words again and again. Wine helped to dull the thoughts running through his mind, but not enough. More might stop them completely. He knew that if he were separated from Judith, if she were to marry another, he would find her and take her back, at any cost. Could he expect any less from another? Did she have a lover somewhere among the host? And who could he be? Rauen? Rauen had been in Judith's company mere days, and yet Griffon had lost his heart to her when first he had seen her. The pitcher of wine at his elbow was empty, he called loudly for another.

~ * ~

Judith's plan, now fully formed, was ready to proceed. She had noticed that late each night, Fionna, one of the kitchen girls, visited Elan, the guardsman who was stationed at the bottom of the Guard Tower stair. She would bring him a pitcher of strong beer from the kitchen. Elan would drink off half the pitcher quickly, then leave the remainder of the pitcher on the bottom most step of the tower stair, there to await him while he enjoyed Fionna's ample favors.

It was a simple matter to slip silently down the stairs, wait until he and Fionna were otherwise engaged and sprinkle a liberal dose of the powdered Monkshood into the beer. Normally used to treat the symptoms of colds, Monkshood had the added side effect of making one drowsy. A large enough dosage would put even a large man into a sound sleep. True to the pattern Judith had noted, after dallying with Fionna for what seemed like an eternity, Elan took up the pitcher and finished it off. Fionna never stayed long in the guardsman's company, fearing discovery. Judith settled down on a step, just past the curve of the stair, to wait. Before long, she was rewarded by deep, sonorous snores coming from the foot of the stair.

Judith had dressed with care for her escape. A deep blue gown, which would appear as a dark shadow in the moonless night. Over that a dark mantle, the hood drawn down over her face, fell fully to the floor. Getting out of the castle without being seen would be the most difficult part. Once outside, Judith hoped that anyone seeing her would mistake her for Aguaine. They were close enough in height.

Judith stayed close to the stone walls, moving quickly from shadow to shadow. Before she knew it, she was out of the Keep, down the stone stair and moving quickly across the Inner Ward without raising a challenge. She had only to cross the outer bailey and exit through the tower gate to effect her escape. It occurred to Judith that Lord Connault should know just how easy it was to move about his grounds without being noticed.

Once outside the castle grounds, Judith moved silently along the outer wall of the castle until coming to the next tower. She dared not proceed any closer to the cliff edge in the almost total darkness in which she found herself. While the darkness certainly worked to her advantage to escape the castle, for the rest of her journey the darkness would bring danger, at least while she moved along the cliffs edge.

Now that Judith's plan had succeeded to this point, she was a little nervous about proceeding with the rest of her plan. She was by now, well aware of the dangers of the road. A woman traveling alone would be an easy target for any number of predators, two legged or four. She was determined to get to Aguaine and nothing was going to get in her way. Aguaine would know what to do about Griffon's insane jealousy. Aguaine would advise her. She would travel as far as possible this night, then, if she had not yet reached Aguaine, she would hide until night came again to minimize her risk. Setting her jaw, Judith set out into the dark, moonless night.

Eighteen

The next morning Griffon sat head in hands, nursing a head that seemed fully twice its normal size. The wine he had consumed the previous night had done little to improve his foul mood and the short time it had dulled the demons was little compensation for the enormous headache that now threatened to split his head in two. For all that, Etaine's words still ran through his mind, tearing at him like a small animal with very sharp teeth. Had Judith found a lover? Was it Rauen? He could find no peace.

"I will kill any man who would take her from me."

"Hard words you speak into the fire, son. What troubles you? I thought you happy in your marriage to Judith?"

"That I love the woman and will marry her, there is little doubt, my Lord. As to happiness, I know naught of the word."

"Brother, I find it impossible to believe that this is the same man I saw just a fortnight previous, laughing and telling all who would listen of his joy.

"Rauen! I have loved you as the brother you call yourself, but I can not abide your company at present. Out from my sight lest I draw upon you."

"Ah! I take it then that she has spoken to you. I feared you would be concerned for her future at first, without land as I am, but this, that you would think me unworthy! I thought, in the end, you would welcome the news. There is naught I would not do for her. My place with Brennus is secure. I can give her a future. And Griffon, my heart is taken by her, there can be no one else for me."

"Out of my sight. To hear you speak words of love about one I hold so dear, it is all I can do not to draw upon you as you speak."

"It is I who brought Rauen here, Griffon. As your father, as your liege, I want this matter ended. I know naught of this talk of love and ladies and do not know what has caused this rift between two men who have been like brothers since the age of five years, but it will end now."

It was Rauen's turn to speak and the pain in his voice was clear, "All these years I have called you brother and you have spoken of me the same. And now I find that I am unworthy to call you brother in fact. You cut me deeply, Griffon. Very well then, I lay breast bare for your sword, for I tell you truly I can not live without the lady, nor can I bear to lose you as my brother."

"I will not draw swords with you, Rauen, not here in this way. If you wish to take Judith from me, then do it by challenge, as the law dictates."

"Judith! What nonsense do you speak? It is Triona, you fool. It has always been Triona who has my heart, Griffon. I thought she had spoken to you."

"Triona, but you were seen in the orchard with Judith."

"Gossip! Judith was but playing the part of sister and chaperone, that I may ask Triona of her feelings for me, before going to Connault to ask for her. The lady is innocent, Griffon. Moreover, she sees only you when she looks to her heart. Who is this carrier of tales, there you will find the source of your troubles. Look again at Judith with your heart, not through eyes clouded by idle gossip. What say you, brother. Have I your blessing, and yours of course Lord Connault, to take Triona as my wife?"

Lord Connault lifted his new son-in-law to be in a great bear hug, all the while bellowing for wine to seal the betrothal. Griffon could not contain his joy, pounding Rauen on the back, then embracing Rauen himself as soon a Connault had released him, nearly crushing ribs in his enthusiasm.

"Rauen, mayhap the day will come to pass that you will find the heart to forgive the black thoughts of this fevered mind and allow me to call you brother once again. But, for now, forgiven or not, I would welcome you as clansman."

"Griffon, I neither ask for nor want apologies, though forgiveness is readily given. It would require more than a

few harsh words to turn this brother's love away."
Throwing his arm around Griffon's shoulder, Rauen, too
called for wine all around. "You know, Griffon, it is not I
you should ask for forgiveness..." Rauen winked at
Connault. "It is the lady whose forgiveness must be
sought, and whose wrath must be met."

"Aye, Griffon, and be prepared to eat your humble pie
with a large spoon." Connault and Rauen both shoved
Griffon in the direction of the Guard Tower.

He could hear the two of them clanking goblets and
laughing loudly at his expense as he approached the tower
where he had sent Judith just two weeks previous.

When Griffon entered the Guard Tower stair, he found
Judith's morning tray lying untouched on the bottom stair.
She had not been down to fetch it. Did the lady sleep late?
An uneasy feeling began to creep into his thoughts. As he
mounted the stair, two steps at a time, Griffon's feelings
of disquiet grew ever greater until he reached her
chamber. Empty!

Griffon searched the small chamber thoroughly over
and over again until he realized that he was looking into
places she could not possible be. Gone!

~ * ~

By the time Judith reached the edge of the forest and
had found the trail she hoped led to Aguaine's small stone
rath, the sun had begun its ascent. Her flight must surely
be known at Dun Tirlough by now. Griffon would have
the entire castle out looking for her. Though she had
originally intended to hide herself until night fell again,

Judith felt panic rise. She must reach Aguaine and decided to continue in spite of the risks.

It did surprise her some that she did not become lost in the dense woods. She seemed to remember every tree, every rock, and when the narrow trail seemed to vanish beneath the shoulder-height ferns, Judith continued without hesitation. Soon, she came to Aguaine's small dwelling in the shadow of the granite cliff. A small brown figure stood at the entrance, waiting.

"Come child, it was time 'e was 'ere."

Nineteen

"You honor me with your visit, my Lord. Your first, since sending me to the tower."

Griffon winced at the sting of sarcasm in Judith's greeting. It was only by chance that his search for her had brought him close to Aguaine's dwelling. He had thought to seek help from his old grandmother in finding Judith, now three days missing.

His surprise at finding her here was equal to his dismay at her sharp words. He was angry that she had run from him, not giving him the chance to tell her he no longer questioned her fidelity, that he knew she was blameless. Angry that she had forced him to search the countryside for her, fearing that at any moment he might come upon her lifeless body. He had lived in constant terror these last three days.

But the anger did not last, it could not hold onto him. His relief at finding her alive, safe, and here with Aguaine, was too great. He caught her up in his arms, burrowing his face into her sweet-smelling hair.

"I thought you dead, lost to me forever. I know I have brought hurt to you and so many others, through my dark moods and jealous rages. No more, I swear to you, it will happen no more. Return with me, my love. Forgive me, my wife."

When Judith had finally found Aguaine, she had been distraught. She pleaded with Aguaine to help her convince Griffon that his jealousy was unfounded. Aguaine had told Judith she need not do anything to help Griffon find his way out of the darkness he had lived in for the last three years, only be prepared to forgive him. Aguaine told her that she would find Griffon changed when next she saw him. It was true, the pain was gone from his eyes. He felt different to her, seemed no longer on guard. Griffon had found peace.

She had spent the last three days in Aguaine's company, learning many of the old woman's ways with the herbs and plants. There was much more for her to learn, but that would be for later. For now it was time to return to Dun Tirlough, time to be married.

"Take me home, Griffon."

Griffon returned Judith to Dun Tirlough and Judith returned to the old chamber she had shared with Triona. It would not be for long. There was little time to prepare for the wedding that was to come.

Great quantities of food would be prepared, for there would be clansmen from far and wide who would come to see Griffon's bride. And to see if the challenge would be met. One of Lady Boann's serving women found Judith in the Great Chamber, next to the fire, trying to make straight stitches in a piece of linen.

"I will never get this right!" Judith tossed the offending piece of cloth onto the bench beside her.

"You are wanted in the Lady Boann's chamber, Mistress."

Her relief at being released from such a tedious task was so great that Judith nearly ran for the stairs. There she found Boann and Triona waiting for her. The look on their faces said they had a secret and were consumed with it.

"All right, out with it. What is this secret that has you both bursting?"

"Not a secret, a surprise."

They parted to reveal the most beautiful gown Judith had ever seen lying on the bed. Touching the beautiful fabric gently with a trembling hand, she couldn't wait until tomorrow came. Tomorrow, the day she and Griffon would be married.

~ * ~

The day of the wedding, Triona and Boann both were needed to help prepare Judith. The gown was a deep blue-green watered silk, which fit tightly across her hips and belly, accentuating every curve. The sleeves, which had to be attached separately, fitted tightly at the wrist, partially covering her small hands, then blossomed out into voluminous folds of luscious silk. The surcoat was fashioned of rich green brocade shot through with gold thread. Slit on each side from hip to hem, the garment fell just short of the floor to reveal the gown below it. When laced, the surcoat fit so tightly, Judith could hardly breathe. However, the effect was startling—her already small waist was cinched to a hand's breadth, the neckline of the coat was scooped low, and cinched in tightly, so her breasts seemed to swell up over the top with soft folds of the silk undergown draped over them. The sleeves of the surcoat opened from shoulder to elbow and again from elbow to wrist allowing the rich silk of the gown beneath to be seen. Tiny seed pearls were sewn all over the lavish brocade surcoat. Around her waist was hung a girdle of intricately carved bronze disks, each set with inlay of highly polished coral and jade, woven together after the fashion of chain mail. Held up only by the swell of her hips beneath the tightly cinched coat, the belt fell from her waist in a softly curved V, accentuating her full hips. A matching necklace was placed about her neck.

Triona brushed Judith's hair until it shone. Tiny braids along each side of her face were pulled together at the back of her head, holding the wave of blue-black hair back from her face, a transparent veil was draped over her hair and face, and held in place by a delicately carved circlet of bronze.

Boann held up a highly polished silver mirror for Judith to view the effect. She did not recognize herself.

Griffon was to meet her at the foot of the tower stair to escort her into the Great Hall. Judith was unaccountably nervous.

"What if he doesn't like the way I look? Perhaps he will not like the color of the gown. My skin is so dreadfully pale," she said as she pinched her cheeks savagely.

Taking Judith's hand in her own, Boann was uncharacteristically tender. "Go, child. Do not make you husband wait. You could not possibly be more beautiful than you are right now." Boann's gentle push propelled Judith in the direction of the stair, which she descended into Griffon's arms. The look on his face told her she need never again doubt that he loved her.

As they entered the great hall, all heads turned to see the bride. They crossed directly to the table where Connault sat with Mog Ruath on his right hand. On his left, where the priest Adolphus was to be seated, the table was notably empty.

Twenty

As Connault rose to speak, the gathered nobles grew silent that their warlord might be heard. Before Connault's first word was uttered, a voice called out from the entrance to the Great Chamber.

"Hold! " All heads turned, an excited buzz ran through the assembled host. A tall blond man stood at the entrance to the Hall. He was dressed in full body armor and came armed into the chamber.

"I challenge this marriage. This woman belongs to me."

"No. It is not true." Judith placed her hand on Griffon's arm, which had strayed to his dagger. Judith felt her heart sink, just when Griffon had seemed to come to grips with his jealousy, this had to happen. Griffon silenced her with a slight movement of his hand.

"You are the lady's husband, sir?" Connault's voice commanded an answer though the words were phrased as a question.

"Nay, Lord Connault, I am Oengas of Bruig na Boinde, the lady's lover and it is at my feet lies the cause of the lady being turned out by husband and family. The deed was done while I was away, not knowing 'til now what had become of her. I come with intent to make right that wrong which has been done to this lady."

Again, Griffon silenced Judith with a motion of his hand.

"Say on, sir."

"I have come to give this lady my name, which is her due, as we have been like husband and wife. If you will but turn her over to me, I will see to her comfort. She is mine by right."

The thin smirk that marred the man's otherwise handsome face turned Judith's blood cold. A very real fear clutched her heart and wrenched at her insides. Would Griffon abandon her now that this man, who was a stranger to her, had for some unknown reason laid claim to her? Who was this man and why did he come here now and say these things about her?

"What say you, Griffon?" Again, Connault's great voice rose over the din that was building.

"Griffon, I must speak to you," Judith pleaded with him. Tugging at his tunic, Judith tried desperately to gain Griffon's attention. She must make him understand that she did not know this man. She knew it was impossible for this man to have been her lover, but Griffon did not. Knowing his jealousy, she feared that this would turn him against her forever.

"Hush," he spoke low so that only she heard. "I swore to you I would no longer doubt you, and I do not. This man lies, but I would first know why." He then raised his voice so all could hear.

"I have but one thing to say, my Lord. This man is one of two things. He is an ill-bred boor who would dishonor a lady's name in front of this assembled company to further his own gain, or he is a liar. Mayhap he is both. In either case, he is a man without honor. It is easily proven."

"Sir, I protest, I have come to honor the lady and make an honest woman of her."

"By slandering her name? I think not. If in fact you truly were the lady's lover, it should be but a small thing to prove. Name that sweet fruit my Lady has borne upon her body since birth and lays promise to the sweeter fruit it would bear."

"I confess, sir, I do not understand. You speak in riddles. Speak plain that I might answer."

"A lover would know, riddle or not, that the lady bears a strawberry birthmark in a place where only a lover... and husband would know it." Judith felt her face grow warm with embarrassment, as Griffon continued, "I will not honor you by taking you to the field of challenge, we will have done with this now. Will you defend yourself, sir?"

Drawing his sword, Griffon moved Judith away from his side.

To everyone's surprise, Oengas did not draw his sword. Displaying his empty hands before him in the age-old symbol of deference, he spoke again, but not to Griffon. "I will not risk death for you, Etaine," he said, turning to the Druid priestess, who was caught in the act of edging toward the entrance to the Great Hall. "You said he would cast her aside once he had evidence of infidelity. You said he would not fight for her."

Two of Connault's guardsmen had appeared at either side of the priestess and, at a signal from the old Lord, they escorted Etaine to the Guard Tower. Mog Ruath hurried after his daughter and her guards. It seemed she was to occupy the tower rooms that Judith had previously occupied. The stranger was led away as well. Both to be questioned later.

Griffon turned to Judith, "My father and I felt there was a chance Etaine would attempt something like this. Her repeated attempts to turn my feelings away from you suggested that this would be her next move. We were ready for her."

"Then you knew from the start that this man was an imposter?"

"Judith, I knew from first I lay with you that you had no lover before me. It was the thought that you might take a lover here, now, that drove me nearly to distraction. That man could not have been your lover... your reason for your leaving your husband. You were a virgin when I first lay with you, therefore, I was certain that it could not have been because of a lover that you had been cast aside."

Banging his cup repeatedly against the table and bellowing for silence, Connault would be heard. "Too long has this moment been delayed. As sat down in the laws of the Brehon, before the Gods and this company, and as is my right as head of this clan, I pronounce that these two are joined in marriage. Now, let us get on with the celebration."

As Connault made his pronouncement, a slow hush spread through the assembled kin of the clan Connault. Heads craned to get a better look at what had caused the sudden silence. Slowly, the crowd that had gathered at the entrance to the Great Hall began to part. A tiny form entered through the cleared passage. Aguaine! In her hand she carried a garland made of mistletoe, blossoms of broom, oak leaves, and meadowsweet. She leaned heavily upon a staff of yew, carved over with fairy faces and magical symbols and wrapped about with the silver branch of an apple tree.

Without a word to anyone, Aguaine approached Judith and Griffon. Taking Judith's left hand and placing it in Griffon's, Aguaine loosely wound one end of the garland about their clasped hands; once, twice, three times, then wound the garland about the couple themselves; again, three times. She removed the apple branch from her staff, fashioned it into a circlet and after first discarding the bronze circlet, placed it upon Judith's head, then tapped the stone floor lightly three times and pronounced so all could hear.

"The Goddess, Danu, has brought together these two before her to be wed. It is the will of the Mother..." Here, Aguaine cast a thoughtful eye towards Connault, "it is the will of the Mother that these two be joined."

This was the ritual she had expected, Judith did not know how or why, but somehow it seemed right to her that this was how she and Griffon would be joined. And she much preferred it to her first wedding experience. Although she and Peter had been married in church, it had been a dry and dismal affair. Neither of them had had family attend the ceremony; Peter hadn't wanted the bother of a large wedding. The only guests had been two college friends of Judith's, who had also served as witnesses. If it weren't for them serving in that necessary capacity, she doubted Peter would have allowed even those two to attend. She realized now that this should have served as a warning of what was to come in her short, terrifying marriage to Peter Ryan.

The feasting began. Platters and trays appeared one after another. Griffon hovered protectively over his bride, urging her to eat, drink, constantly filling her goblet with sweet wine. Then came the music. Three traveling musicians, faces painted to resemble masks, sang songs only of love, happiness and contentment as befit an occasion of marriage.

Judith's head spun from the wine, the music, the attention, until she could barely think. Presently, Boann, Triona, and the nobles' wives came to lead Judith away to prepare her for her husband. She hadn't the heart to tell Boann that she and Griffon had already consummated their marriage. *Well, Griffon had let that secret out in front of everyone in the clan, at the marriage ceremony, hadn't he.* Judith guessed there wasn't much point in pretending. Apparently, Triona had read her thoughts, for she winked wickedly at Judith, making her blush.

When Griffon arrived at their chamber, accompanied by a host of his clansmen, he found his bride already beneath the thin linen coverlet, her shining black hair arranged in a cloud upon the pillows piled beneath her head and shoulders. The thin sheet hid little, clinging softly to the swell of breast, belly, and hips. He shut the door with finality upon the grinning faces of his kinsmen and turned his own grin upon his wife.

"Always you seem to grin at me in a most boyish manner, My Lord."

"I feel most boyish in your presence, My Lady."

"Then come to me, husband. Let us see what we can do about that."

Echoes of laughter followed the puzzled well-wishers as they descended the tower stairs.

Twenty-one

The next morning, Judith awoke to bright sunlight shining through the eastern facing loop. Smiling to herself and remembering the intimacy of the previous night, she turned to Griffon but his place beside her was empty. She sat up, wondering at his absence, to find him just coming through the entrance to their chamber.

"You're up early."

"The day is well begun. As much as I would enjoy spending the day abed with my wife, I had need to see to the questioning of our guests in the guard tower."

This statement got Judith's full attention.

"What did you find out?"

"The man has confessed that Etaine hired him to challenge me. He was to convince me that he was your lover. She hoped I would not believe your protests. Then he was to take you far from here and leave you by the road somewhere."

Judith shuddered at the thought, drawing closer to Griffon. And yet, for some reason, this confession did not satisfy her.

"It doesn't make sense, Griffon, what of the attempts on my life? Did he confess to those as well? Why would Etaine make two attempts to take my life and, when she had me within her power, leave me somewhere in the wilderness? Why not kill me and be done with it?"

"He claims to know nothing of these attempts. I believe he speaks truthfully for he is a stranger to us and would have been noticed at a time when we were looking for a stranger; an assassin. Etaine must have made those attempts herself, bringing this man in only when she found she could not get to you in the tower. Perhaps he was unwilling to commit murder and leaving you by the road at the mercy of the vermin there would effect the same results without actually welding the blade himself."

"Why Griffon? Why did she do these things? Did she say anything about her reasons for doing this?"

"Etaine was betrothed to Ciran when they were both very young. When my brother died, it seems she could not give up the idea that it was she who should be the next Lady of Dun Tirlough. Bryon had been wed to Annu within days of the news that Ciran was dead. In truth, it would have been unseemly if Etaine had wed another so soon after Ciran's death. When Maeve died in childbirth, she conceived of a plan to be wed to me, then she felt she could manipulate me into challenging Bryon upon our father's death. Under Brehon law, any male kin may challenge to inherit, even if the family tie goes back up to five generations. She felt that Aguaine would support my claim, which would carry much weight with the people. Then of course, her own father would know the law and uphold my right to make the claim."

"But why kill me? Why would she try to kill me? It seems to me that to attempt murder first, then to fall back on this plan to carry me off somewhere and just leave me does not make sense."

"I do not know. She will not speak of that. Also, she admitted that she told the stories about Maeve because she wanted me to hate the child, Mairead. She planned to give me children and believed that if I did not already have a child I loved, these children of hers would increase her hold over me."

"Her plan would not have worked." Judith stated quite simply. "I know you well, Griffon. You are not one to be led about by anyone and I do not believe you would ever have challenged Bryon."

"You are right, it was a foolish scheme. I believe Etaine to be unbalanced. She spoke many evil things during her questioning. This has broken her father, he is an old man, and Etaine is his only child. I fear he will not survive it."

"Is it over now?"

"For us, yes, my love, it is over. We are free of her."

"Good, then I shall dress, we will pack food and the three of us will ride into the forest for a picnic."

"Three? What three?"

"It is time you knew your daughter. Mairead will accompany us."

The passage of an hour found them at Clonmacconaul. Judith snuggled against Griffon as they watched Mairead run through the meadow gathering wild flowers. Judith had given over her favored spot in front of him on his horse to the child and had been rewarded by the adoring looks Mairead had bestowed upon her father. She had watched as the long neglected child blossomed under the sudden attention of the father she had not been allowed to know. Griffon, too, had been deeply affected by the sudden contact with the child he now knew was his own. She had seen the long withheld love of a father for his child bloom before her eyes. For the first time, he allowed himself to experience fatherhood.

She watched with delight as Griffon chased Mairead across the meadow, roaring like a dragon, to squeals of excitement from Mairead. He would catch her up in his arms and swing her far overhead and she would beg for more.

And now the play-weary child slept soundly in her father's arms as they returned to Dun Tirlough. Boann and nurse met them at the steps and took the exhausted child to her room.

That night Griffon and Judith lay in each other's arms, equally exhausted, though for much different reasons. Griffon nuzzled Judith's neck, playfully rubbing his beard stubble against her cheek. He brought up the subject of children.

"I missed much of Mairead's infancy. We should perhaps have a babe of our own soon."

"What's this? Are you not jealous of the time I would have to spend tending to a baby?"

"The time would be well spent, and nurse would help."

Laying his hand upon her stomach, Griffon spoke seriously.

"Etaine robbed me of my daughter's childhood. Cheated Mairead of the father she deserved. I will never forgive her that. Nor can I escape blame myself. I willingly accepted the lies she told and turned my back on the child my own eyes should have convinced me was my own. I have only you to thank for giving my child back to me."

"And I have one more thing to give you, Griffon. It is not certain, but I believe that I am carrying your child."

"Truly?" Griffon pressed his face against Judith's stomach, making her giggle.

"Do you hear me in there? This is your father. I make a vow to you that you will never be denied the love and care of he who has sired you."

"Come here to me, Griffon." Judith opened her arms to him. "I would have my husband make love to me."

"As you command, Lady."

Twenty-two

In the small hours of the morning, Annu's baby entered the world. Griffon and Judith awoke to frenzied excitement. Bryon had at last been roused from his contemplation and he nervously paced a small path before the massive stone fireplace of the Great Hall. Griffon, Connault, and Rauen slouched in various chairs and benches as they took up the vigil with their kinsman. Triona sat quietly on a bench beside the fire. It was not proper for an unwed maiden to attend upon childbirth. Judith assumed Boann and the other married women of the household were with Annu and, feeling a need to be helpful, she and Triona brought a steady supply of food and ale to the waiting men. Then she too took up vigil on a small stool close by her husband's side. As the hours passed, she became more and more certain that tragic news approached. And so it was with trepidation she rose to face Boann when finally she approached.

"It is a difficult birth, the child is breech. Annu rests now. Soon I must return to her."

"Boann, let me return with you. I know I have little experience with childbirth, but I can help. I can fetch and carry for you. Help to walk her." Judith felt she would lose her mind if she didn't have some activity to occupy her mind and hands.

"No child, it is best you do not."

Puzzled, Griffon followed Boann from the room.

"What is it my Lady Mother? All women are needed to help in a birth. Judith has just told me she suspects she is with child herself. It would be good for her to know what is to come."

Taking her son's arm, Boann led her son still further from the group huddled by the fire. Griffon noticed the concern in his mother's face and grew fearful himself.

"Griffon, already the Christians among us tread softly around our Judith. They have marked her as one to be feared. If anything should befall Annu or the babe, Judith would be blamed. It is best that she should be elsewhere. You know that Adolphus would use any excuse to take up the cry of sorceress yet again."

"Mother, you of all should know that many babes are born in silence, never to take that first taste of their mother's milk. How could this death be laid at my Judith's feet?"

"Son, Annu is not right," She said, tapping the side of her head.

"She speaks nonsense mostly; raving of demons and hellfire. Midwife but mentioned Judith's name and this sent Annu into fits of raving, calling upon this God of hers to protect her and the babe from Judith, whom she calls 'Satan's whore'."

"You are right, of course, my Lady. It is best to keep Judith well away from Annu and the babe until all is well."

"By the by, my son, Judith is quite correct. She is with child. Connault and I are to have another grandchild. I can see it in her face. Odd it is that I can see it so clearly so soon after the wedding night." Boann gave Griffon a rather pointed look, raising one eyebrow questioningly, but said no more.

Boann left her son to return to the birth chamber, carrying with her an arm full of fresh, sweet-smelling reeds that had been collected recently for just this purpose.

Griffon did not tell Judith of Boann's fears. He would not have anything worry her or harm their child. Why should she worry about this? Instead, he told her of Boann's certainty of the child she carried. They sat together on a bench near the fire, talking in whispers of the child they would soon have. They would remain at Dun Tirlough until their child was born. Griffon would make use of this time to prepare his own manor for his return with wife and child. Presently Mairead was brought in by her nurse and ran to Judith and Griffon.

When Boann returned she found Bryon still pacing. Connault and Rauen discussed plans for he and Triona. Connault would make them a gift of Clonmacconaul where they might build their home after their marriage. Along with the meadow would come several hectares of land. Though Rauen was a younger son and would not inherit, he would be landed, thus furthering his position in Brennus' court. Griffon and Judith had too been gifted with land, which ran adjacent to Griffon's own.

Griffon sat by the hearth and watched Judith and Mairead. Judith had a bit of yarn and was teaching Mairead to play 'cat's in the cradle'.

Boann's approach brought them all to their feet.

"The child did not live. It was a boy and he fought bravely to be born but by the time the midwife delivered the child, the cord had wrapped about his neck. Annu has been put to bed, Bryon, she asks for you."

Bryon wandered off, looking about him in his dazed manner.

Judith's fears confirmed, she sought Griffon for comfort. Now fully aware that she too would soon face childbirth at a time when little was known of medical care, she was more than a little concerned for herself and her child. Her firm belief that this was merely a dream brought on by delirium did little to comfort her. Real or not, she belonged here and that other place, where she had come from, was becoming less and less real; more of a dream than this place.

Griffon was not comforted by the look that passed to him from his mother. There was a silent vow understood by each that Judith must be protected from any potential harm that might come of this.

Twenty-three

To the surprise of both Griffon and Boann, the following succession of days passed in relative quiet. Each day, before rising, Griffon would inspect his wife for signs of the coming child. Each day Judith would laugh as his face showed his disappointment at her still flat stomach.

"Griffon, it is much too early to show anything at all!" she would admonish him.

"But, I wish to see your belly swell. To know that my child lives there within you."

"My 'belly' will swell soon enough. And will be swollen for far longer than I wish to think about just now. So, please, do not wish for it any sooner than necessary."

Griffon would spend his mornings at practice with his men. The afternoons he would spend with his father, deep in discussion over the affairs of the country. Bryon had withdrawn deeper still into oblivion. Annu drifted about the Keep like a spirit, avoiding all save the priest, Father Adolphus. She would wander from her chamber to the chapel and back to her chamber. If someone should chance upon her, she would pull back into a shadow until they passed.

Judith spent her mornings with Boann learning the workings of a large Keep. She also worked at increasing her store of medicinal herbs and plants. Connault had set aside a small plot of ground in the orchard gardens where she might cultivate some of them. Her days were busy, and contented. But always she would save time for Mairead, who was her joy. Late mornings, she and the child would carry a large pitcher of ale to Griffon upon the practice field.

~ * ~

The household began to take on an air of anticipation as the Festival of Beltaine approached. This pagan festival was a celebration to welcome summer and would take place three days hence. Food must be prepared, festival clothes aired and made ready. The open grounds that stood outside of the curtain wall began to sprout tents, as clansmen from all over arrived.

The day of Beltaine, a huge mountain of dried wood, very nearly the height of one of the smaller towers of the Keep, grew upon the cliff's edge from a base so large it would take twenty and five grown men standing hand to hand to encircle it. Come that evening the towering brush would be set ablaze.

Judith and Mairead stood hand in hand watching the men build the great mound of wood when a gnarled brown hand reached out to tug at her sleeve. Startled, Judith whirled about.

"Aguaine, you are here. How wonderful to see you again."

"Aye, it is a most special Beltaine this year. He who is to be Lord of this land will be wed with the Goddess in her earthly embodiment, to ensure the fertility of the land and the welfare of the people."

"Do you mean Bryon? Aguaine, Bryon is a Christian, I doubt he will even attend this festival, let alone participate in any ceremony."

"He who has been chosen by the Goddess to rule will do what is expected when the time comes."

With a knowing wink and finger placed beside her nose Aguaine would say no more, but seemed content to stand and watch with Judith and Mairead. Mentally Judith attempted to calculate the old woman's age. She knew that Boann had been her first child conceived at the Beltaine ritual. She had probably been about fifteen years old. Boann herself had been married at fourteen and was now forty-six. Judith was shocked to realize that would make Aguaine only about sixty-one or sixty-two years. Not old by twentieth century standards. Judith turned to ask the old wise woman if she knew her great grandchild, Mairead, only to find she had slipped away, as silently as she had come. Puzzled, she looked about but did not see the tottering old form anywhere in sight.

~ * ~

One hour later, one of the guardsmen brought a frightened and tearful Mairead to the Keep in search of Griffon. He had found the child wandering through the multi-colored tents crying for Judith and her father. Calmed by Griffon, who fought to hide his own fear from the child, Mairead said a 'big man' had approached the two as they watched the men build the bonfire and he had told them that Griffon had been injured and he had been sent to fetch them. He had led them a short distance toward the forest when Judith had suddenly become suspicious and drew back. The man had grabbed Judith and dragged her into the woods, but not before Judith had called to Mairead to run to her father. Mairead had turned and fled.

Kissing the child's small cheek, Griffon told her what a clever child she was to have remembered all of that. He passed her to Boann and an agitated nurse then ran for his waiting horse. The guardsman had already called upon the men of the Keep who awaited Griffon's orders.

He had only one. Find his wife.

Twenty-four

The search continued long into the afternoon. All to no end; there was no sign of Judith. In a desperate attempt to find Judith, Griffon now rode through the crowd of people, Mairead perched in front of her father, hoping she would see the man who had taken Judith. Rauen, Bryon, and Connault rode to each side. It was no use. The child was trying but it was useless. Mairead was returned to the Keep with one of the guards.

The crowd was immense. Everyone from miles around was there for the festival. All began to gather about the bonfire as time approached to light the fire. Tradition held that the Lord of the land would symbolically 'wed' with the earthly embodiment of the Goddess to ensure the land would be productive. Connault had grown too old to uphold the tradition and with Bryon being a Christian, there was little hope of the ancient tradition continuing. Watching Annu's thin pinched face as she made her way through the crowd to the edge of the bonfire, Griffon had trouble picturing her participating in this ritual as well.

"Annu? What does she here?"

"She is well enough, Griffon." Bryon replied "It is good she is out among the people."

"My brother, the Lady is a Christian. A devoted one at that. What does she here at this pagan festival?"

The fire was being lit. Griffon watched Annu's face as the first licks of flame glowed red. His gaze followed hers to the fire as it began to catch the dry wood. He looked back to her face. Horror spread through his soul as he watched her lips pull back from her teeth in some hideous parody of a smile. She looked very much like a demented wolf, snarling over a fresh kill.

Griffon gasped, turning to Connault. "The fire. By the Gods, the fire."

He charged through the crowd, his father, Bryon, and Rauen close behind him. Lugh's great mass scattered people from his path. He heard an inhuman shriek as Annu saw him and realized he knew.

"Too late! Too late! Let the demon's whore burn in her own pagan fires!"

Desperately he rode round the mountain of wood. Toward the back the fire had not yet spread and Griffon thought he saw a pale patch deep within the piled branches.

Flinging himself from the back of his horse, he attacked the dry kindling. He could see her, but could not reach her. Smoke clouded his vision, stung his eyes. It was impossible to reach her. Searching frantically, he at last found what he thought to be that place where Judith's abductors themselves must have entered the stacked wood. Frantically pulling at the tangle of branches, he at last reached Judith at the heart of the mound. The fire had not reached her yet but was quickly approaching. He could hear the roar of the flames in his ears. The smoke watered his eyes. Sea breezes fanned the crackling blaze.

He tried to lift her unconscious body but could not. Frantic, peering through the blinding smoke, Griffon realized she had been staked to the ground so that if she should awaken, she would be unable to escape the burning pyre. He shuddered to think of Judith awakening in the center of this inferno, only to find she was unable to move and unable to save herself.

Quickly he severed the ropes with his dagger. Unable to stand fully erect within the stacked wood, Griffon lifted Judith as best he could and staggered forward, praying to the Goddess he was moving in the right direction. The intense heat seared his lungs, making it difficulty to draw breath. Stinging smoke caused his eyes to tear. Griffon choked back the fear that clutched at him and would have immobilize him. He would not allow Judith, and his child, to die in this inferno. At last, Griffon broke through the maze of branches into clear, clean air.

The astonishment of the people when they saw the young Lord Griffon, son of their own Lord Connault, emerge from the fire with Judith in his arms, turned to cheers and shouts of amazement.

Aguaine appeared from out of the crowd. A path cleared for the beloved old fairy and the crowd quieted as she began to speak.

"The Goddess has chosen. Griffon, youngest son of Connault, has wed with Danu. He is chosen by the

Goddess to lead the people. Connault, many years ago you made a vow to preserve the old ways in this land. You have sired a son who has been chosen by Danu to carry on that vow. That son has married she who was chosen and brought to him by Danu. What say you Connault of Dun Tirlough."

Taking Aguaine's hand, Connault bent knee before the old woman.

"So be it. As set forth for us by the traditions of the Brehon, I proclaim Griffon mac Connault, who has sprung forth from the old race and is chosen by the old Gods, to be heir to this land."

Bryon, too came forward, his head held high.

"Father... my Lord, my heart is much relieved at this news. As you know, it has long been my wish to enter the monastery at Skellig Michael. This desire was put aside in order to fulfill my responsibilities as your heir. I welcome the news that this great responsibility has been lifted from me, one who is so poorly equipped to handle it. My Lord Father, Griffon, I ask only this. Should Judith and her child prove to be unharmed, I pray God this should be so, I ask only that Annu be returned to her family. It is obvious to me that her mind has come to be unhinged. It is equally clear to me that I, and the priest Adolphus, had more than a little to do with this. Myself, because of neglect, Adolphus due to his stories of demons and witches. Back with her own family and in a strictly Christian home, I pray that she might recover her senses. And, of course, Adolphus will be sent away with Annu. I realize that this is much to ask, I beg your forgiveness, both for Annu and myself.

But Griffon was oblivious to the commotion, wanting only to see to Judith who was beginning to regain consciousness. It was Connault who reassured Bryon that, should Judith and the child prove to be unharmed, his wish would be honored.

As Judith opened her eyes, the first thing she said to Griffon was, "We must return to the Druid well, Griffon. At once."

Twenty-five

That very night they started out on a journey back to the Druid well. Judith had insisted they could not delay. Through the night and all the next day they had traveled. Griffon was very worried about Judith and the child. She would not rest, would not say why they traveled to the well, only that they must.

Her obsession grew as they neared the Druid grove. When finally they reached the well Judith was near to panic.

Finally, they stood beside the sacred well of the Druids.

"Griffon, it was at this very spot that I stood and prayed to Danu to bring me to you. I did not know at the time that it was you I prayed for, but she did. She knew. I made an offering, a small thing; a simple gold chain. When I awoke, there you were. She has brought me all that I prayed for; you, a family, a home to belong to and now a child.

But, I have allowed the memory of where I had been to grow dim. I began to assume that I could remain here with you forever. I forgot something very important. I forgot to give thanks. I feel it deep within me that this will all be taken from me if I do not acknowledge and give thanks to She who gave you to me. I feel myself becoming insubstantial, as though I might disappear at any moment."

"Why did you not speak of this to me before we left Dun Tirlough. I would have brought gold plate, silver chalice. I would have brought with us something fitting to give as thanks to Danu."

"No. Only a simple gift from the heart. This is all that is needed."

Without hesitation, Griffon removed the ring he wore on his left hand and, taking Judith's hand in his, they approached the well.

"Never was my life complete until you gave your love to me. I will thank Danu for the rest of my life for this gift she has given me."

He let the small offering drop into the well. Taking his wife into his arms, he said, "Come, my Lady and my life, let us return home. We have a long life to begin."

Epilogue

Present day Ireland

"Professor Ryan!"

Peter Ryan heard his name shouted over the tremendous din of the storm. He and Lord Donnelly, along with several of Donnelly's retainers, had been searching for Judith since she had run from the cottage into the teeth of the storm three hours earlier.

"Over here, Professor Ryan. This way."

Ryan was frantic to find Judith. His anger at her had not diminished. Once he had her alone, he would deal with her disobedience. However, his anger at her was not so intense as his growing fear that she might let it be known what had happened between them that night. The violence of his attack on Judith had filled him with power and yet it had also frightened him; his mind had seemed to go to a place it had never before been. Now, because of this momentary lapse, because he had acted in haste, his entire career might be at risk. It was unthinkable to him that this *woman* he had married might be allowed to mar his impeccable reputation.

Peter reasoned with himself that this did not make him as cold-blooded as it seemed. After all, wasn't it his responsibility as Judith's husband to make sure that she received the proper training as a wife? In his own way, he did have some feelings for her. Perhaps he would relent, and allow her to have a child.

"Peter, this way. We may have found something." Colum's voice came to him over the roar of the wind.

When Professor Ryan finally found his way to Lord Donnelly, he found his old friend and several workmen crowded around the newly excavated well. Several stones were missing from the side of the well. Perhaps his problems were to be solved for him.

"Over here, Peter. One of the men spotted something at the bottom of the well and we've lowered him down to have a look."

Something was shouted up from the bottom of the well but the constant screaming of the wind made it impossible to hear what the man said.

When they had hoisted him back to the surface, the man was alone and the look on his face seemed to tell the story.

"Sorry, your Lordship, I would have sworn that I saw her down there. It must have been reflection from the lamps. At any rate, I only found this, my Lord."

Into Lord Donnelly's hand, the man placed a thin gold chain. Threaded on the chain was a man's silver ring with polished stones forming the image of the mythic Gryphon. Lord Donnelly had placed the very same ring into Judith's hand for inspection just that day, the same ring that Colum Donnelly clearly remembered Judith returning to him.

Except, the ring Colum Donnelly had excavated from the well had been tarnished and corroded by time and the elements. This ring was clean and polished as though just this moment removed from the owner's own hand. Absentmindedly, he touched the pocket where he had placed the ring when Judith had handed it back to him. It was not there. He searched his pockets carefully. Inspecting the ring closely, he would have sworn it was one and the same ring.

"Excuse me, your Lordship. We searched the grove thoroughly. She just isn't here. Where could she have gone on foot, by herself, and in her nightclothes?" Lord Donnelly's workman looked decidedly uncomfortable about the words he had just spoken. His meaning was clear.

The mystery of the rings momentarily removed from his thoughts, Colum Donnelly viewed his old friend through new eyes. Concern creased his brow. "The fellow's right, Peter. Where could she have gone? It is you who directed us to search the woods. She clearly is not here, nor is there any sign of her." Lord Donnelly seemed to weigh his next words very carefully. "What exactly did you and Judith fight about this evening?"

Meet Katherine McGibbons

I've been a storyteller all my life, beginning at age seven when my little brother decided he didn't like the way his bedtime stories always ended the same way. So I began to create new endings for the old stories. Before long we had abandoned the old favorites altogether and I was creating new stories especially for him.

As a teen I wrote short stories, but they were just for me; it never occurred to me that anyone else might be interested in reading them.

After a while, work and life got in the way, and it wasn't until I reached my forties that I started to write again.